OTHER BOOKS BY
JILL SYLVESTER

YOUNG ADULT FICTION
The Land of Blue

NONFICTION
*Trust Your Intuition: 100 Ways to Transform Anxiety and
Depression for Stronger Mental Health*

DEVON: DREAM AGENT

AWAKENING

JILL SYLVESTER

OLD TREE HOUSE
PUBLISHING

AWAKENING
BY JILL SYLVESTER

Old Tree House Publishing
Copyright ©2020 Jill Sylvester
All rights reserved.

Old Tree House Publishing
PO Box 462
Hanover, MA 02339

This is a work of fiction. Names, characters, businesses, places, events and incidents are either the products of the author's imagination or used in a fictitious manner. Any resemblance to actual persons, living or dead, or actual events is purely coincidental.

Editor: Rebecca McCarthy, www.thewrittencoach.com
Copyeditor: Jody Amato, jodyamato@gmail.com
Cover and Interior Layout: Yvonne Parks, PearCreative.ca
Proofreader: Clarisa Marcee, www.AvenueCMedia.com
Author Photo: Maura Longueil

Publisher's Cataloging-In-Publication Data
(Prepared by The Donohue Group, Inc.)

Names: Sylvester, Jill, author.
Title: Awakening / Jill Sylvester.
Description: Hanover, MA : Old Tree House Publishing, [2019] | Series: Devon: dream agent ; [book 1] | Interest age level: 012-017. | Summary: "Devon struggles with crippling dreams that have plagued her as far back as she can remember. It isn't until she hears a voice calling her name though, that she realizes the dreams are becoming reality. She wishes she could talk to her father about all of it--her dreams, her anxiety, her mother's death when Devon was five, and the nightmare that ended up coming true--but her father refuses to discuss the dreams or the details surrounding his wife's passing"--Provided by publisher.
Identifiers: ISBN 9780998977539 (paperback) | ISBN 9780998977546 (Kindle) | ISBN 9780998977553 (ePub)
Subjects: LCSH: Teenage girls--Juvenile fiction. | Mothers--Death--Psychological aspects--Juvenile fiction. | Nightmares--Juvenile fiction. | Anxiety in youth--Juvenile fiction. | CYAC: Teenage girls--Fiction. | Mothers--Death--Psychological aspects--Fiction. | Nightmares--Fiction. | Anxiety--Fiction.
Classification: LCC PZ7.1.S95 Aw 2019 (print) | LCC PZ7.1.S95 (ebook) | DDC [Fic]--dc23

DEDICATION

To those who trust in the power of their dreams
and who follow the dimly lit path to awakening.

"Who looks outside, dreams; who looks inside, awakes."
CARL JUNG

CHAPTER ONE

"Devon," the voice whispered in the darkness, sounding neither near nor far.

My eyelids flashed open, my back sweaty against the flannel sheets, the cardboard-tan, masculine-looking set Dad had bought at Target. Fragments of a dream faded from my conscious mind—a room, small, adobe-grey, like walls in a cellar, a car crash, red car, compact, a girl with rosy-apple cheeks, hair matted against her head, like she had just been asleep, scared. I remember she looked scared.

Who called my name?

I lay there stiffly, with shallow breaths, feeling the images slip away from me, disappearing into the larger space of my bedroom, my eyes darting back and forth, trying to remember pieces of the dream, like a puzzle I was being timed to put back together.

I had never heard a voice before. Usually it was just the dreams that woke me from sleep. Was it a message? Was I going to be in a car crash or something? Was the voice male? Female? I couldn't tell. Gram? Mom?

Sweat dripped from the back of my bony knees onto the sheets, as I realized I could no longer remember the sound of my mother's voice.

My heart clambered against my chest, each pounding a desperate attempt to get out of my body. Could it have been my mother? Or my grandmother? Was that even possible?

I threw off the covers and sat upright in bed, hugging my small frame to keep the huge feelings locked inside. Who had called my name? Was it some kind of warning? Did I imagine it?

I dug my short fingernails into the sides of my upper arms, through my red short-sleeve Gap T-shirt. These weird things I did always made me feel better for some strange reason, like pressing, pinching, or digging into my skin, hard enough to feel pain. Hard enough to feel something for real, I guess. I had been doing it for a long time, ever since the bad dreams started, back when I was little. Though the bad dreams were different bad dreams then.

Pulling myself closer, my toes indenting the mattress, I tried to breathe in and out through my nose, the way they taught us in that yoga workshop at school, whenever the Warrior Two pose got to be too much. It was no use.

With my arms wrapped around my shins, I glanced over at the small, square silver clock on my bedside table: 2:30 a.m. The clock sat in front of the porcelain round-bellied lamp, like a baby kangaroo inside its mother's pouch, beside the cylinder container of Calm, the product that was supposed to—according to my dad's latest girlfriend—help me sleep through the night.

I dug my nails harder into the previous grooves on my slender arms that had yet to heal, matching the pain to my fear. I didn't imagine it. Someone had called my name. Was it a bad spirit or something? But why would a bad spirit come to me? I didn't do anything wrong. After what happened with my mother, I never would.

The sound of a car whizzed by outside my window. I tried to remember if the voice sounded bad, or felt bad, or if I could see a color associated with it, but I couldn't. I just knew for sure that I heard it, as real as if someone had stood beside my bed and uttered the words. The word. *Devon.* Except no one was there.

I curled my toes deeper into the mattress, causing them to cramp. Was I being warned? Or was it a message for someone other than me?

I swallowed hard. I wished I could wake Dad. But I couldn't. Would there ever be someone who'd explain this stuff to me?

Unable to move, I sat in bed and stared out the front double windows with the half-moon transom, making our one-level ranch house in Hanley, Massachusetts appear fancier than it really was. I caught the taillights of a car driving past, a swooshing sound on the pavement letting me know it had rained during the night. The red glare reminded me of the colors.

Instinctively, I rubbed my eyes with both fists, deep in their sockets, until the fireworks appeared, swirls of fuchsia and blotches of violet bursting behind my tired eyes, the way they did when I was younger. I used to imagine the bright hues erasing the scary images I often saw in my mind, an ethereal etch-a-sketch. News stories like house fires, the war in Afghanistan, and segments from *COPS* that Dad liked to watch after work bombarded my dreams in my pre-teen years until Gram, in that gentle way she had, told Dad she didn't think I should be watching certain programs at my age, that it might be causing my nightmares. After that, we switched to my then-favorite shows, *Family Feud* and *Hannah Montana*.

I pressed my fists to my chin. Now, in the first semester of my junior year, I felt too old to believe I could obliterate the dreams from my memory. The things I saw now, I knew, didn't come from the television.

Another car drove past, in the opposite direction on Kingston Road, its headlights illuminating the wall across from my double bed, highlighting the grey sweatpants hanging over the footboard, and the navy-blue Cape Cod sweatshirt—the one I got in middle school when I spent the weekend with Gwen and her family down the Cape—slung over the baggy sweats.

My hands still balled into fists that now clutched at my waist, I felt my stomach tie in a knot.

The freaking SAT!

I had to be up in four hours! Sweat dripped from under my bra, the one I wore to bed after I showered, so I could simply get up in the morning and go. How was I supposed to take a test, *the most important test*, after only a few hours of sleep? That's all I had heard from the Health and Wellness teachers over the years—how sleep was so important for teens, and if we didn't get enough—the standard eight-plus hours a night—we'd have lower test scores and increased anxiety. Maybe that was my problem, in addition to the other ones.

My body trembled, the way I imagined an earthquake began, reminding me I had no control over my life, that I didn't fit in with the other kids my age whose sole concern was the SAT—the benchmark for worth, the measurement tool for college placement—the test that made me feel stupid when I heard other students scored 1200 on the PSATs on their first try.

I pressed my nails into my skin, making a half-moon shape near my shoulder. Did I even belong in college? It's not that I wasn't smart—my schedule a mix of honors and standard classes—I did fine. I just didn't compare to kids who obsessed about scores in the conversations I overhead during class and at lunch, spending so much time talking about the schools they wanted to get accepted into, like they knew where they wanted to go, for certain. I wasn't sure I was ready for college, or that it was the place for me, the way everybody else seemed to know, and that made me feel worse about myself, as if they all knew something I didn't. I mean, how could you really know, at not even seventeen, what you wanted to do for the rest of your life?

The bottom of my bed creaked, the way Dad said mattresses sometimes settle, when I was younger and thought there might be a monster under my bed. I bit my thumbnail. I just didn't want to disappoint my mother. I heard my mom had been smart in high school. But she had gotten pregnant with me the summer after graduation, changing her plans to attend a state school, forced to make different decisions. I wondered now what my mother would want for my future.

The clock ticked. 3:00 a.m. My brain throbbed, the way the bass in my dad's F-150 beat loudly in the driveway after he'd come home from a date.

I leaned over and switched on the lamp and then pulled the round, wooden knob of the drawer of my bedside table. Mine, but not mine, really. All the furniture in the room had been Dad's when he was growing up. When my parents got married, a few months after the news of my impending arrival, my dad's parents gave them this house, one of two rental properties my grandparents owned in town. They're not rich or anything, they just own Alante's, a family-owned auto-body shop and gas station in the center of Hanley that my dad and his brother, my Uncle Rob, took over after my grandfather passed away, before I was born. Being teenagers, my parents didn't have much, so Avo—my dad's mother—let them take my father's old bedroom furniture, which is great and everything, it's just that the bed, the bureau, and the bedside table were all Dad's. I wished I had something that belonged to my mother.

I shimmied my journal out from the narrow side table drawer to write down my dreams, which I usually did when I needed to go back to sleep. The medium-sized journal, with its purple and pink mosaic cover and matching Pier 1 pen, was the most feminine item in the room. I liked the rough feel of the tiny green, pink, and purple beads on the twist-off cap of the pen, the color scheme resembling the swirl I often saw behind my closed eyes.

Sometimes I observed colors the same way, but with my eyes open. It's hard to explain. The colors I saw—well, more like *felt*—gave me information about a person or a situation, classifying someone or something as either good or bad. This was another one of those weird things. It made me feel different to know instantly, by the change of a color in my mind, whether I could trust someone or if they didn't give a damn about me. Like the chick who dated Dad for almost a month when I was in middle school and ended up keying the side of his beloved pickup truck when she found out he was also spending time with another woman in town.

The first time I met Ho #57—as Frankie and Gwen and I liked to call her—a dark green color seeped into my mind space, the way sewage looks at the bottom of a trash barrel. I never told Dad, though, that I felt the 30-something-year-old bar troll was bad news, or that information even came to me that way. I never told anyone, really, except Frankie and Gwen—my two closest friends from the neighborhood, my only friends really— who considered the color thing pretty cool. Mostly, I kept the expression of that subject—my dreams and the weird way I experienced things—limited to the pages in my journal.

I slid my feet closer to me, my pajama shorts scrunched to my hips, my bare knees pointed toward the ceiling, creating a desk on which to write. The lamplight flickered. A chill ran through me and I glanced around the room, as if the person, the spirit, the thing that spoke to me might show up again, this time in form.

A bead of sweat ran down my chest. I turned toward the back of the light-blue-lined pages of the book, the one Gram had given to me a month before she died, the summer before I entered eighth grade. When I felt like I couldn't talk to anybody else, she said, when it felt like nobody understood, *write down your feelings.*

I looked down at the other, untouched pillow beside me, and then tried to find where I last left off, flipping the pages of my past. I noticed words of the other nightmares that had woken me and of the feelings surrounding my mother's early death, Dad's voice programmed in my mind, "Hold your head up, girl. You're an Alante."

I tucked the left side of the journal under the right, obscuring the entry dated nearly two months earlier, August 16:

> *Frankie's hanging out with the football idiots again now that practice started.*

I felt my stomach tighten as I stared at the blank, right-sided page. Frankie and Gwen would always be my best friends, even if Frankie was more of a social butterfly now than he ever was before, when it was just the three of us growing up in the neighborhood.

I scrawled October 5 across the top of the page with the bumpy pen.

> *I heard a voice. It scared me, the same way the dreams about that little girl scare me, and all the other random ones about people I don't know. It makes me wonder if part of me is crazy. Seeing things, now hearing things. Isn't that what happens to crazy people? Why do I see bad things? I don't want to feel crazy during the most important year*

of high school, when I'm supposed to be preparing to enter the real world. Actually, I don't want to feel crazy ever. I need a sign, Gram, to know you hear me, and that God hears me, if He's listening, and that I'm not crazy. And I need to sleep.

Clutching the pen in my hand, I scanned the room one last time, yawning through half-closed lids. The wall creaked in the far corner of my room, near the front window. Silently, I prayed nothing would happen the rest of the night.

I tucked the journal back in the drawer, pulled the covers to my shoulders and slid down into my bed, hoping to get a few hours before the harp alarm sounded on my cell phone.

Closing my eyes, lid to cheek, my heartbeat slowed to a gentler rhythm as I curled under the covers, continuing my conversation with Gram. *It's like someone's trying to tell me something, trying to get my attention,* I thought, in that half-sleep state.

Maybe someday I'd understand.

CHAPTER TWO

I slowly opened my eyes, wondering why there was so much light in my room. Something was wrong.

Groggy, I turned over and checked the ticking clock. 8:45.

Shit!

I flung back my covers, causing my nicely organized, put-out-the-night-before clothes to fall into a pile on the floor. Did my alarm even sound? I leaned over and grabbed my phone, where I kept it plugged in behind the headboard. Texts from Frankie and Gwen filled the home screen.

I slung my head back and covered my hands over my face. *WTF!*

Goddamn voices and dreams.

Frankie's 8:13 a.m. text read:

Dude, what's up!!! I'm afraid to beep in case your dad's still sleeping. Old Man Coleman's been eyeing me through the side of the window shade for ten minutes. He's lucky I don't flip him off. Sorry my friend, but I gotta go. Don't get mad! I texted you five times!

Blood rushed to my face.

F*** overslept,** I replied with both thumbs. **Call me when you're done.**

Frankie, my ride because Dad usually headed to the shop on Saturday mornings around nine and I didn't drive yet—another weird thing since I'd be seventeen in December and hadn't even signed up for driver's ed. Dad just drove me places, or trusted Frankie and Gwen—who got their licenses the minute they turned sixteen and a half—to drive me to school, to work, to the shop. With the aftermath of car accidents my Dad witnessed at Alante's, the main auto-body shop in town, you'd think my father wouldn't want me to get my license, but it was my doing, or not doing. My dad already taught me to drive, so I knew I could, I just didn't want to. The thought of driving on my own made me nervous— especially now after the dream about the car crash— and wasn't high on my priority list, unlike taking the SAT to see where I stood compared to my classmates and if I had a shot at a decent future.

I quickly removed my cotton shorts, tossed them on my bed, and grabbed the oversized sweatpants off my floor, yanking up each leg one at a time. With flailing arms I pulled the sweatshirt over my dampened T-shirt, and then tugged on the two white ankle socks I had originally placed side by side on the light blue carpet next to my bed.

I abruptly opened my bedroom door, accidentally banging it against the wall beside my closet. I turned right, down the pale green, matted-down hallway carpet leading to the kitchen, never even bothering to step into the bathroom across from my bedroom and glance at myself in the tiny mirror. The smell of toast and bacon filled the kitchen, Dad's typical breakfast after a Saturday morning workout in the basement.

"Why didn't you wake me up?" I snapped, my voice still raspy from sleep as I planted my size five-and-a-half feet onto the cream tiled floor.

Dad looked over his shoulder, standing in front of the sink in his white V-neck T-shirt, as he poured bacon grease into a bowl, straight from the frying pan. "Huh? What do you mean?" Then, "There's bacon there if you want it." He jerked his head toward a paper-towel-lined plate on the island counter, several pieces of golden-brown turkey bacon cooked just the way he liked it.

"What do you mean what do I mean?" I asked with my hands on my hips, my hair wild around my head. "I had the SATs, Dad! Don't you remember?"

"Oh, shit, I forgot," my father said, sort of looking at me as he cleaned the frying pan with one of the Brillo pads Avo faithfully kept stocked under our sink.

I yanked open the refrigerator door with my slender arms. A tiny dancer's body, Gram used to say, "a petite doe," even though I had never taken a dance class in my life.

"Was Frankie pissed?" Dad asked, drying the pan with the faded red-and-white dishtowel that had previously been draped over his shoulder. "Did he even beep the horn?"

"It's not Frankie's fault," I said, raising my brows before I slammed the refrigerator door, opened the cabinet next to the sink and brought down one of the plain black mugs from the lowest shelf, setting it on the counter next to the orange juice with a bang. "Most parents remember to wake their kids up for a test that means *everything*."

Dad chuckled while he put away the dry pan in a cabinet next to the stove filled with old black and stainless steel pots and pans while I poured myself a drink. "Frankie probably didn't want to wake me after a late night."

"Frankie was sick of freaky Mr. Coleman eyeing him through the window," I snarled over the rim of the mug.

"I told you guys a hundred times, Mr. Coleman's harmless," Dad said, wiping his hands on the towel and then tossing it beside the sink. "And can't you just take that test in the spring? What's the big deal, anyway? I got you set up at the shop after graduation. You'll help Uncle Rob and me, just like we did for my dad. You can take community classes or whatever, at night if you want. We already talked about this. I gotta keep the business in the family, and you're my only offspring . . . that I know of, anyway." Dad winked.

I shot my father a look as I gripped the mug harder with both hands. "That test was important to me. To *me*! It's important for every junior who wants to plan their future!"

Dad took his phone out of the pocket of his sweatpants, his go-to for avoiding conversation. "Look, I gotta get into work. You know that. Stop making this a bigger deal than it really is."

I placed the half-finished drink on the island counter, next to the daily *Boston Globe*, the sports section separated from the rest of the thin Saturday paper, tears forming in my eyes. I blinked them back, pressed my thumbnail into the pad of my index finger, visualizing Gwen and Frankie, and the rest of my peers, pencil to test sheet as the microwave clock glowed 9:20.

Dad sighed, set his phone down next to the stove. He rubbed his forehead and then rested his hands behind him on the strip of laminate, unglued in a few spots, bordering the sink. "C'mon now, don't give me a hard time. I didn't know it was my job to wake you. You have your phone, right?"

Yeah, I have my phone, I just don't have an involved parent, I thought to myself as I stared down the front hallway toward the welcome mat next to the front door, where my navy-blue Nike sneakers sat, ready to go. I wished I could say to my father, *I slept through the alarm because a voice woke me up in the middle of the night.*

Dad's ringtone sounded at a medium volume on his phone, Outfield's "I Don't Wanna Lose your Love Tonight," a song he liked in his younger days. I wondered if the voice I heard was trying to get me to remember the dreams I had from last night, or the other ones I've had, for a reason. Was the voice even good? How do you know if a voice in the middle of the night is good or bad? I didn't get a color or have any feeling on that. I stepped my right heel down on the top of my left toe and gave it weight.

I wanted to say these things to my father, who spoke on the phone to Freddy, one of his mechanics. I wanted to have a conversation about the dreams, the same way we talked about the SATs, and my dad's plans for me to work at Alante's, even though I couldn't stand making small talk with the customers—not to mention the notion that my father could have some other kid from some other female. But I couldn't.

My father finished his conversation and shoved the phone in his back pocket, searching for his keys I could see hidden under the newspaper. "What if I wanted to go to school, like a decent school, not just community college? I'd need the SATs to get me in, you realize that, right?" I said, squeezing my upper arm through my sweatshirt, pretending to scratch an itch.

My father snapped on his silver Citizens watch, the one that made him look dressed up when he went out for dinner. "I don't know why you care so much about going to college when there's already a job waiting for you. I know people who would love to be in that position." With his heavy, tree-trunk thighs, Dad trudged past the island and over to the oak cupboard standing between the basement door and the front hallway, looking for the keys he usually kept in the pale-yellow, oddly shaped ceramic bowl I had made for him in second grade, the one that sat on the main shelf of the cupboard, underneath the glass cabinets housing plain vanilla-colored dishes and cups from the Christmas Tree Shop and above three rows of drawers filled with take-out menus, business cards, and other paperwork Dad stuffed into the bottom drawer.

I pressed my foot into the toe kick heater at the bottom of the island. "It's just that what if I wanted to see if there were other things I could pursue, you know, discovering something I might be good at? Do you ever even consider there might be something else for me?"

Dad pushed the straw-covered end chair of the six-seated, dark wooden kitchen table farther underneath, the table my parents purchased in the hopes of entertaining someday, the table that now seated only Dad and me, and occasionally Avo when she stopped by after dropping dinner off for us, still, a few times a week. "You're good at lots of things, Dev," my father said, gripping the spindles of the chair, "mostly being a good daughter. Everyone likes you at the shop. You've grown up there and you do a good job with the paperwork when we ask you to help. Why wouldn't you want that full time? I know you don't like talking to everybody who comes in, but don't you wanna help Uncle Rob and me?" Dad moved aside the napkin holder, and them mumbled, "Where the hell are my keys?"

I stared at the shiny silver ridge of one of the three keys on his set, sticking out from under the front page of the paper. I pinched the fleshy part of my left hand, between my thumb and first finger. "It's not that I don't want to work for you. I just don't know for sure. I don't know if that's what I am supposed to be doing! I feel like there should be options."

Dad scratched at the back of his head, the way he did when he had somewhere else he needed to be. "I don't know. I don't think of things that way, all right? I graduated high school, good football player, but no grades. That's just what I did. I went to work for my family and it's provided me with a good life, just like it'll do for you." Dad rotated his shoulder, the way he did when he felt stressed. "Don't make things more complicated."

I cracked my knuckles. Avo always swatted at my hands when she saw me do that, telling me I'd get arthritis. "What do you think Mom would have wanted me to do?"

Dad leaned his head to the left to crack his neck. "Your mom's not here. I'd like to think she'd want you to work for me and have a good life. Look, I don't think that test means much in life, okay? I didn't go to college and I'm doing good. Now, I gotta go. I gotta find my friggin' keys. I'm already behind the eight ball."

Blood rushed to my cheeks, flushing my medium-toned skin. "You always have to go," I mumbled under my breath.

"What'd you say?" Dad asked, his face tilted, his eyes small.

"I said, 'There's your keys.'" I raised my brow, my voice sarcastic as I pushed the newspaper aside. "Meanwhile, this was a big deal for me, my future is a big deal *to me* and you act like it's nothing!" I crossed my arms over my chest.

Dad swiped the keys off the counter, never looking directly at my face. "Look, it was a late night. I can't deal with this drama right now. I'll let you know later if I have plans with Tina."

With half-closed lids, I watched as my stocky father stomped down the hallway, grabbed his black Adidas zip-up jacket from one of the front hallway coat hooks and stormed out the front screen door, slamming the heavy wooden door behind him as he left.

You're right, Dad, I thought, standing alone in the kitchen, my body weak from lack of sleep. *It was a late night for me too.*

CHAPTER THREE

At 12:30, my phone buzzed.

Frankie texted:

SATs sucked. Just got to Panera with Gwen. We'll walk over after I drop car to Janice. Meet in the tree house?

Frankie's text a reminder that I hadn't yet eaten, I got up off the couch to have some of the sausage linguiça Avo had dropped off yesterday afternoon.

I placed a paper towel over my plate of homemade food and slid the dish inside the microwave, the clanking sound interrupting the quiet. Dad always worked on Saturdays, even after being out late on a Friday night. The nights I occasionally did go out with Gwen after work, Dad still got home later than me.

The microwave beeped. Twice. I opened the door, pulled the plate of food out and set the hot dish on the counter beside the sink, my phone buzzing in my pocket. I read the text from Gwen:

Up to going to game with me later?

I slid my phone back in my pocket.

I had hoped Gwen would want to stay in and watch a movie with me, since Dad would most definitely be going out, and Frankie would be going out after the game with the football team to some party I had no desire to attend.

Gwen and I really hadn't been able to talk much during the week, since our shifts at Holly's usually involved Holly standing right behind us, making sure we cleaned every drop of ice cream from the counter. Gwen also had a boyfriend now, this kid Andrew she met last May down at the beach.

Taking a bite of food, I glanced out over the windowsill above the sink that held a small statue of Mary, her hand placed over her heart. "There," Avo had said when she placed the statue there years ago after buying it at the Christmas Bazaar at St. Thomas Aquinas in Abingdale, two towns over, where she played bingo a few times a week. Patting the statue with her thick, olive-skinned hands, she declared in her husky voice, "For good luck."

Through the glass, past the grey-painted deck, the damp leaves mixed yellow and green, tossed like confetti across the lawn. A flash of a red bird flew past the tree house in the very back of our half-acre lot, bordering the narrow strip of woods separating

Gwen and Frankie's houses on Timber Lane from mine. I couldn't tell if it was a cardinal or not—and one of my "signs"— since the dash of red could have also been a house finch.

My grandmother taught me at an early age about the signs—you know, repetitive numbers, butterflies, lights flickering at weird moments, chills running down your spine, that sort of thing. Gram came to believe, "too late in life," she once said, that our deceased family members sent us messages from Heaven through signs—messages intended to let the rest of us remaining in the physical world know that our loved ones still existed, albeit in a different form. Before she died, my grandmother told me she'd communicate with me in the form of cardinals, due to her "gorgeous red hair." Since then, I see cardinals pretty much everywhere.

I crossed the tile floor behind the kitchen table over to the backslider door. I slid off my socks and pulled on the oak handle, hard, with my left arm, the fake plant that Avo's friend Eleanor had given Dad after he had been running the shop for ten years collecting dust on the floor. Above the plant, a white shelf held a stack of knit dishcloths that Gram had made, which Dad found useless.

I stepped barefoot out onto the deck, sliding the door closed behind me, the air brisk and chilly against my face. The bird feeder on the deck was still halfway full, despite the New England air growing colder. I tucked my hands inside the sleeves of my sweatshirt, my phone tight against my right wrist, and trudged down the two grey, damp wooden steps to the backyard, hoping I'd catch a better glimpse of a cardinal from the tree house.

Crossing the yard, my feet crunching the leaves, I reached the bottom rung of the wooden ladder leading to my beloved tree house. Grabbing both sides, I climbed up, feeling the familiar wood under my feet, knowing where to step, avoiding the splintered pieces. I crawled through the opening and toward the back, my sweatpants gathering at my knees, across the faded red, blue, and green braided rug cradling crumbs of Doritos in its little grooves from all the late-night talks over the years with Frankie and Gwen. Finally, I turned, pressing my back against the wooden slats in order to view the entire yard stretching out behind our grey, shingled ranch. The green canopy top overhead protected me from the elements when I'd lay up there on summer nights, watching the stars. I even brought my pillow out there sometimes, falling asleep on several occasions.

The wide, dark wooden tree house "comfortably fit four," Gram boasted the day the company assembled it when I was a little girl, a gift given to me by her, my maternal grandmother. I guess I had said that I wanted to see my mother in Heaven. I remembered Dad scanned the tree house after the workers finished the job and said that fifteen feet off the ground, we could get real close to the sky and to Heaven.

A chipmunk scampered across a nearby tree branch, causing a few brownish-green leaves to fall to the ground. Dad only spoke that way when I was young. My father didn't believe in the signs, the way Gram did. I remembered one time he came home for lunch during the days when Gram watched me after kindergarten, and he stroked the back of my head with his sturdy, grease-embedded hands while Gram and I squealed because a red dragonfly had landed on my arm. Closing one eye, Dad pretended to survey the crabgrass-filled lawn from our back deck, a toothpick dangling from his lips, his brown work boots heading back inside a moment later through the slider doors to return to work, without uttering a word.

Dad didn't talk much about the signs, or about my mother, as I grew older. When your wife takes her own life, with a combination of vodka and pills, and whatever else she imbibed that late afternoon nearly twelve years ago, leaving behind a five-year-old to care for, maybe that's a hard thing for a guy to do.

CHAPTER FOUR

Below, the crackling of twigs and leaves crunched and snapped.

"Ouch!" Gwen winced.

I heard Frankie first utter "Sorry," as my two neighborhood friends traipsed through the overgrown path. Then, "I can see her, she's up there."

Frankie Ricciardi, Gwen Davidson, and I had known each other since we were old enough to walk the short path behind my house on Kingston Road to the cul-de-sac where Frankie and Gwen lived, three doors apart, on Timber Lane. It had pretty much been the three of us from elementary school up to now, the fall of our junior year. We preferred it that way, never really bothering with the idiots in the neighborhood, like Sydney

Cummings and her cheerleader snob friends, or Keith Hughes, who basically had been selling weed since eighth grade.

We weren't losers or anything. We just didn't run with the popular crowd at Hanley High. Which was fine with me. I never liked big groups of people. I'd much rather hang out with people who knew me, and my dad, and our situation, like with my mom being gone and stuff like that. And even though Frankie had been venturing out more with his football friends and Gwen had been spending more time with her good-looking, ripped boyfriend, the three of us kind of had this thing—you know, that we'd always be there for each other, having known each other from the neighborhood.

Back in second grade, the three of us thought we were so cool because we got to walk, without parents, through the woods to each other's houses. It felt comfortable to me now, like a worn-out pair of Gap pajamas, and we were still doing the same thing junior year. "I'm here," I called over my shoulder through the slats. Frankie and Gwen pushed past the now-only-green forsythia bushes and fought to get to the ladder first. Old habits die hard.

"Do you have any manners?" Gwen barked, as Frankie clambered the ladder in front of her. "I never noticed how immature you are, first you whack me in the face with tree branches and then you cut in front of a girl to go first, which still matters to me, if anyone cares in this political climate." Gwen shook her head in disgust and then scaled the ladder with her 5-foot, 7-inch lean frame, fit from years of playing tennis at her parents' club.

Frankie paused on the top rung, sticking his smallish butt in Gwen's face before scrambling through the opening. "That's what you get."

"Oh my God!" Gwen laughed and smacked Frankie's behind. "Remind me of the benefit of our friendship?"

"I make you laugh," Frankie said, his agile cat-like body scampering beside me and sitting against the right wall of the tree house. "I also put up with your complete bitchiness, which is worse, by the way, now that you go out with real-life Gaston."

Gwen ducked her head inside the opening and crawled to the opposite side, facing Frankie and me. Turning and sitting crossed-legged in her black and white Lululemon outfit, Gwen wiped the dirt from her freshly manicured hands. "So, what's going on? Why did you miss the test?"

Frankie adjusted his royal blue Panthers cap more tightly on his head. "Did you have another dream?"

I pulled my knees into my chest, my eyes still red-rimmed from my argument with my father.

"Don't ignore me," Frankie warned, hitting his knee against mine, sounding like the brother I didn't have.

I rubbed my toes together because the whole thing still made me feel weird, even among my truest friends. "Sorry, guys, I just had a really bad fight with my dad. You'd think he'd make sure I was up for the SAT. Like, know my schedule and care about it," I said, before I bit down on my lip. "Anyway, yeah, I dreamed something about a car crash maybe, but nothing I really remember. Except that I heard my name called, like someone was standing there, but obviously they weren't. It freaked me out."

Gwen raised her perfectly shaped brows. "Ahh, that would freak *me* out. Unless," she added, leaning into my space and squeezing my right shoulder, "it was your Gram."

"Still," Frankie said, his eyes bugging out as he shook his thick, wavy brown head of hair that resembled a bird's nest.

"Yeah," Gwen said, sitting back in her spot, as if she thought better of it. "Still."

A blue jay chirped in its irritable way on a nearby branch. "I couldn't tell if the voice was nice or not nice. I know that sounds really weird," I said, pulling my knees closer to me.

Gwen nudged her foot against mine. "Maybe you're psychic. I definitely think you have something. My mom said so too, after that time you dreamed Livvy made herself puke in middle school, even before we all knew she had an eating disorder."

I rolled my bottom lip. "Yeah. That was random. I just don't get the point. Why do I keep waking up? Like if it was a message or something, what is it? And is it for me or someone else?"

A simple sparrow flew low across the yard. "They say that psychic ability runs in families," Gwen said, adjusting her position on the bumpy rug that ran under her legs, her butt on the hard wood, "like from grandmothers who read tea leaves."

"I'm pretty sure Avo never read a tea leaf in her life," I said, pursing my lips.

Gwen closed one eye and clicked her teeth in agreement. "But what about Gram?"

I shook my head. "No. I mean, she taught me to pay attention to the signs and everything, but whenever I had bad dreams, she got really upset—she didn't offer me any words of wisdom or anything, if that's what you mean."

"Maybe you got this from your mom," Gwen said, twirling the two silver rings on her left hand with her turquoise-colored nails.

"Yeah," Frankie said, while he checked out his lean, newly toned arms after a couple months of football. "Drugs can make you see all kinds of weird shit."

"And you know this because?" Gwen asked, her head tilted, looking like a reporter minus the microphone in her hand. I stared at Frankie, without a word.

"Not me, you idiots, I'm just saying, I've seen people on some bad stuff and you know, with all due respect, your mom had anxiety," Frankie knew all the mental health terms since his mom, Janice, worked in the psych unit at the local hospital.

"That has nothing to do with the dreams," I said, my stomach clenched like a closed fist. "Or my mother's depression and anxiety. Please tell me you don't think this is all in my head. I know what I heard this morning."

"Dude," Frankie said, leaning over his criss-crossed legs, "all I'm saying is, if your mom had anxiety you know, you could too."

"The dreams do make you anxious, don't they?" Gwen asked, her forehead scrunched.

"I guess so. Wouldn't you be?" I asked, with widened eyes. "I want to hear how you guys would feel if your name was called in the middle of the night, or if you had constant bad dreams. I don't think it's because I have some anxiety disorder like my mother had." I pressed my heels hard into a groove in the rug.

"No, you seem too cool for an anxiety disorder. I, on the other hand, would definitely be a mess," Gwen said, tightening her ponytail. "I totally require eight hours of beauty sleep a night."

"I didn't say you have a full-blown anxiety disorder," Frankie said, rubbing the top of my shoulder. "You know that girl Ashley in middle school, who always ticked in gym waiting her turn in dodge ball? She probably has GAD. That's Generalized Anxiety Disorder to you schmucks. Anyway, it's just that the dreams mess you up, Dev. You overslept for the SAT! That's causing dysfunction in your life." Frankie used air quotes to convey his point, the sleeves of his navy blue and gold Hanley windbreaker falling just past his bony wrists. "It's also a full moon, dude. Janice says the unit's stocked whenever there's a full moon. I dunno, maybe you just need to knock yourself out at night, with some CBD oil or something."

"And I think maybe you should re-evaluate who you're spending time with these days," I said, raising my brow.

"I agree," Gwen said, straightening her back against the side of the tree house. "I don't want to hear that you're taking part in any drug stupidity."

"Easy you two. Jesus, it's like having three mothers instead of one who's already up my ass, no dis to Janice. Anyway, this is about Devon." Frankie stretched out his stick-like legs covered in grey sweatpants in front of him, and crossed his feet at the ankles.

"What about talking to someone?" Gwen asked, while she pulled at her earlobe, just underneath the diamond studs her parents gave her for making National Honor Society. "Maybe that would help."

"Like a therapist?" I asked. I could see PJ Alante's reaction to *that*, the man who preferred to "keep things in the family."

Frankie nodded, his cap pulled halfway down his forehead. "Maybe a good shrink'd help you analyze the dreams, figure things out and shit. Dude, a therapist has clout."

"Clout, now there's someone who's ready to take the SAT," Gwen stated, raising her still slightly tanned finger in the air.

"Yeah, and still probably scored less than 1150," Frankie said, as he pulled the rim of his cap down tighter on his head.

This should have been the norm. The SAT. Planning for college tours, keeping up with the latest on social media, parties and other stuff I considered nonsense. Maybe I could take local classes if I did end up working for Dad, if I decided not to go to a real college, but then, wouldn't that make me kind of a loser? Not that I really cared what other people thought. It's just that other than Frankie and Gwen, and my father, I didn't really feel like I belonged. That right place that felt like I was supposed to be there. Did every kid my age long for that? Or was it just me?

"You guys really aren't making me feel better," I said, resting my chin atop my knees. "I don't want to start thinking that this is just anxiety messing with my head. I know what I heard. And I know what I see in my dreams. I just don't understand why."

"Well, you have to do something," Gwen said, twisting her hair into a bun. "You look tired. You *are* tired. And you missed the test! That's not like you. You're Miss Organized. The one who lines up every color of sprinkles in a row when we've already signed out from our shift. You're better at that than you are at talking to the customers, for God's sake."

The sky shifted, the autumn afternoon sun settling behind the tree house, creating a column of sunlight in only one section

31

of the yard. I wondered if my mother had friends, like I did, to talk to when she felt anxious.

"And Devon's right, you do need some new friends," Gwen said, her green eyes on Frankie. "Some of the football guys are cool, and cute, but the ones you hang with are annoying. Couldn't you pick ones higher up on the food chain? The way Joey Mosley belches like Elf after lunch makes me want to throw up every single time. I swear."

"Since when are you up on social status at school?" Frankie asked, jerking his chin. "Last I heard, you couldn't have cared less who was a nobody and who was a somebody. Until you starting dating Gaston, that is."

"Stop with the Gaston. You're one to talk, hanging out every second these days with the football crowd, like they're your new best friends. Jeez, guys, it's not like I've changed that much since I've been seeing Andrew," Gwen said, tucking a strand of straight, glossy dark hair behind her ear.

"Oh yes, you have," Frankie replied, stretching his arms above his head, elbows bent before touching the ceiling. "You're way more girlier, and far more squealier. And don't dis my boys on the team—just cause I was a late bloomer, don't be raining on my parade now that I have some friends other than you guys," Frankie nudged Gwen's leg first, and then my bare foot, with his black and white Nike sneaker.

"I'm *squealier*?" Gwen winced, looking over at me.

"You're definitely squealier," I confirmed, giving Frankie a wink, grateful the conversation had moved away from my possibly having an anxiety disorder. Could anxiety cause nightmares?

"C'mon guys," Gwen said, rolling her eyes. "Where's the support? I like Andrew. A lot."

Frankie straightened his arms out in front of him, his back curved into a C-shape to get it to crack. "Did you do it yet?"

The sun lowered behind the tree house on Timber Lane. Gwen and I snuck a glance at each other in the emerging darkness, recalling a previous conversation after the sophomore dance in June that Frankie wasn't privy to. "I have not, not that it's any of your business. But I will say this—I'm pretty sure he's the one."

"The one for what? Sex or marriage?" Frankie asked, with a smirk.

Gwen pulled on her earlobe. "The one I like enough to do things with."

Frankie slowly nodded his head. "I see how it is—this topic's off limits now that you're 'in a relationship.' That's cool. Just don't lose yourself over some guy who might be a total douche."

"Andrew's not a douche," Gwen said, flicking a mosquito away from her ear.

"Whatever," Frankie said, moving into a kneeling position and then squatting on his heels. "I need to be up at the field soon for the game. You going, Dev?"

Nestled high up above the yard, the tree house burrowed the three of us in, holding space for some of our most private conversations. Our motto: what's said in the tree house stays in the tree house. That included when Frankie had a beer for the first time at a football player's house freshman year. Admitting to wanting to act cool and fit in, Frankie said if we ever outed him to his mother—which of course we never would—he'd deny it. Frankie's mother loved Gwen and me like daughters and probably would have believed the two of us over her only son, no offense to Frankie.

"Nah," I said, biting my lip. "I'm gonna try and get in early tonight."

"Got you," Frankie said, with a nod. "Sleep tight. I'll see you in the morning for our gig."

"If you change your mind," Gwen said, nudging my foot with her black K-Swiss sneaker, the thin raspberry-colored line on her white sock sticking out the back, "Andrew has a really cute lacrosse friend who wants to double-date. Said you were beautiful when he saw my Instagram."

I chuckled through my nose. "Thanks, but I'm good." I wasn't, really. But I wanted to be.

Gwen leaned over, gave me a hug, and then followed Frankie down the ladder to freshen up for the Hanley versus Marshton game, where Andrew went to school. And after the game, doing things I probably should be doing at my age, too—if I was normal.

A lone gray catbird flew down from a nearby oak tree, darting through the diminishing sliver of light on the lawn. As much as I loved my friends, I didn't think they understood. I wondered if out there somewhere were people who felt the same way as me—people who saw things in their dreams and felt different from everyone, the way I did.

CHAPTER FIVE

Later, I filled the silver tea kettle Avo had bought on one of her weekly trips to Macy's with fresh water, preparing to make myself a cup of chamomile tea. I stared at my reflection through the kitchen windows above the sink, the yard outside now dark. I lit the stove, hoping the tea might help me relax, the way it used to when Gram made me a cup. I planned to unwind on the couch the rest of the night alone, since Dad had texted that he'd be out with Tina.

I opened the fridge in search of the familiar yellow-capped squirt bottle of honey, forgetting that the new local raw, pesticide-free honey—care of Tina, who owned the Local Grocer store in town across from Alante's and who also was dating my father—now resided in the sugar cabinet beside the stove, something about preservation at room temperature. A few cans of Heineken lined the inside door of the fridge, beside the Vitamin Waters and Frank's Red Hot, for when Uncle Rob stopped by, or when Dad occasionally wanted to unwind at home.

I shut the refrigerator door. Dad didn't have to worry about me drinking.

After grabbing my journal from my room, my bed still unmade from the way I had bolted out of it this morning, I headed down the front hallway, my left foot on the hardwood, my right foot on the maroon and green runner that stopped a few feet from the front door. Turning right into the living room, I set my half-drank cup of tea, journal, and black-cased phone on the square leather ottoman in front of Dad's recliner.

The speed of my heart beat matched the speed of cars that sped by on the main road in front of our house—people with places to go and things to do—deflating the notion that any kind of tea might help, that I might feel normal, that something might change. I stared in silence for a while, the cars darting past, my mind dizzy with the torrent of thoughts running loose inside my head. Maybe I did have anxiety, the disorder kind.

I sat down on the blue and red plaid couch opposite Dad's favorite chair and with jittery hands took a sip of my now-tepid tea, placing the World's Greatest Daughter mug on the floor beside my feet. I clicked through the channels with the remote, trying to find an episode of *Friends*, my now-favorite show, to serve as company while I read through old journal entries, hoping to find some previously recorded dream that made sense of why someone might have called my name.

Surfing past the local news, a litany of *Lifetime* sagas and movie channels we didn't subscribe to, I couldn't find *Friends*, so I settled on an episode of *Cupcake Wars*, the show Gwen and I used to watch in middle school, when we liked to bake sweets after school at her house. Then I picked up my journal, the stubby pen peeking out of the back of the book, where I had left off this morning.

I flipped back through the pages, sitting cross-legged on the couch, the contestants on the television conversing at a low volume, frantically trying to beat the clock and showcase their skills and talents.

I rested my thumb on the page dated August 3, the words *the little girl* scrawled on the side of the page in the blank space. I looked up and stared out the side window, next to the television, the sheer curtains showcasing the shadowy arborvitaes guarding Old Man Coleman's shingled and badly-in-need-of-a-power-wash split ranch. Old Man Coleman was the name Frankie had given my reclusive next-door neighbor in fifth grade.

I sighed to break the spell, making myself read the entry that had kept me up the entire night two months ago.

A little girl. I couldn't tell how old or anything because it appeared fuzzy and distorted. I think I've seen her before, but I'm not sure. Same girl? Different? I don't know. It scares me, the feeling when I see these people, these girls. It makes me wonder if who and what I see are even real, like my mind playing tricks on me, like what it might be like on drugs. Why does this happen to me? Is it even real?

I pulled my legs in closer to me, the clock on the side table next to Dad's recliner moving its big hand rigidly forward another minute. During psych class last year, Mr. Weiss had said that Carl Jung believed characters in dreams represented an aspect of themselves. That made sense to me. Every time I dreamed of some random girl, trapped in some small room alone, like she was abandoned or something, I suppose she could have been representing me, and maybe the way I felt after I lost my mother.

The next entry wasn't until the following week, the writing scribbled in chicken scratch.

August 10.

I just saw a car crash in my dream. A bad one. A red Prius, totaled. It was so real. I saw the driver, male, squished up against the dashboard, but I couldn't tell who it was. Didn't feel like someone I knew. I don't think they died, but it was a bad accident. A telephone pole, yes, the car hit a telephone pole on the side of a main road, like Route 53, but not exactly, just not a side street, where the speed limit is 35. Maybe alcohol-related? I don't know. A crimson and gold BC High sticker on the back windshield. Why would I see this? I don't know anyone personally who goes to that school. What am I supposed to do, if I don't even know these people? Am I supposed to help somebody in some way?

I pointed the remote to the opposite corner of the room and shut off the TV. Unable to wait up for Dad any longer, I put myself to bed at 10:30.

Lying in the dark, I closed my eyes and took deep breaths, in for three, out for four, an exercise I had found on Google once when searching for self-soothing techniques to help you sleep. Restless, the journal entries forefront in my mind, I turned over, the bottle of Calm Tina had given Dad to help me sleep better staring me in the face. I never tried it, not wanting Tina to be the one to potentially help me solve my problems.

I shifted on my back and tried again—in for three, out for four—my heart attempting to slow down as I realized that lately, the dreams were occurring more often. They didn't happen every night, but they happened often enough.

Enough that they messed up my sleep, messed with my mind, causing me to think about things I didn't want to think about, like car crashes that jolted me awake, as if they were happening to me, as if they might, and girls trapped in rooms, alone. The dreams also messed with my future, causing me to oversleep for a test I needed to take, unlike the rest of my classmates, who had no problem making it on time, probably going to bed with their pencils lined up next to their car keys, their cell phone alarms waking them after a sound slumber.

I clenched my jaw, knowing I needed to sleep, to make up for last night. Was that the purpose of the voice? A warning that I might get in a car crash? Or was the warning that someone else would? If it was a message, how would I know how to help if I didn't even know who they were? Or did I really have some kind of anxiety disorder and this was causing me to lose my mind?

CHAPTER SIX

Thunder cracked and split the humid atmosphere, jolting me out of slumber.

Wide-eyed, drenched in sweat, I watched the lightning illuminate my pitch-dark room.

I gripped the sheets with my right hand, an anchor, the rest of me unable to move.

I remembered my dream.

Except it was more like a movie, a movie I witnessed as if I were standing in the same space, as if I were an extra, not given a speaking role, but definitely playing a part.

Lightning flooded my room a second time.

That girl, the cashier from The Natural Grocer, the sweet, socially awkward one with the matted down hair and the thick-rimmed glasses. Denise.

In a kitchen, her kitchen, someone's kitchen.

A stove on the right side of the room, with a pine-green teakettle on one of the four burners, and a soiled off-white dishrag on the counter, heaped in a pile like it belonged in a restaurant, used to clean off tables for customers. Yes.

Light oak cabinetry, with black hinges, lined the left upper and lower walls, and the closed back door led to a narrow stairway between the first and third floors of the house—the number twelve pulsing in my mind, twelve stairs?—where a man had entered.

My heart rose up into my throat.

A wild-eyed man, with sandy, sweaty hair, wearing a silver skull ring on his finger, had entered the kitchen from that same stairwell and attacked Denise, the cashier—the one who worked for Tina, the one who thanked me three times with her eyes closed, her hands in prayer at her heart, when I told her once that she gave me back too much change. He attacked her with a hammer, in the middle of the kitchen, her body in a heap on the floor.

The guy, who in the dream, at least, felt to me like her boyfriend.

Thunder erupted outside my window, coming closer.

Was Denise dead?

I gasped for breath, my chest heaving visibly into the darkness of my room.

This time, in my dream, I saw someone I recognized. Someone I knew in my actual life.

This time, the dream seemed so real.

CHAPTER SEVEN

I never fell back to sleep.

I stared at the ceiling, covers pulled taut to my chin while the gruesome scene played over and over in my mind, singeing its mark on my memory.

At 8:00 that morning, Frankie beeped the horn of his new, but gently used Jetta—as he lovingly referred to the way the car dealer had sold it to him—in my driveway.

Reluctantly, I got up, still dressed in the clothes I had on yesterday.

With my eyes barely open, I brushed my teeth in the little bathroom across the hall, the rusted radiator against the back wall under the shelf that held two hairbrushes, Old Spice deodorant spray, my light blue container of Secret, and a dark green bottle of Brut. Half-heartedly, I checked myself in the cloudy mirror above the vanilla bean-colored, ceramic sink, wetting the first two fingers of each hand, whisking my naturally medium-brown eyebrows into place. I didn't need much makeup, and I wouldn't have taken the time to apply it even if I did. I never understood the girls who looked like they took forever to get ready in the morning.

I grabbed one of the two remaining blueberry muffins in the Stop and Shop bakery carton beside the toaster. Dad had texted earlier from Tina's, letting me know that he had stayed over and would see me later.

Frankie beeped a second time. I shoved a bite of muffin into my mouth and then washed it down with a quick glass of orange juice. Wiping my mouth with the back of my hand, I wondered why I had agreed to this other job. The last thing I felt like doing after yet another night of interrupted sleep was unloading umpteen containers of shoes off an eighteen-wheeler into a damp warehouse on Sunday morning.

Twelve. The number twelve reverberated in my brain.

What did the dream mean? I thought as I wedged my feet into my sneakers. *Was Denise really dead?*

I shut the front door tight and trudged down the three concrete steps, pulling my light-brown hair, the tips of which ran halfway down the middle of my back, into a messy bun, my tan Old Navy tote bag slung over one shoulder.

"Let's go!" Frankie called.

While I traipsed through a mound of wet green and orange leaves, my eyes instinctively looked past the hood of Frankie's car, through the line of Spruce and Arborvitae trees on the other side of the driveway.

No sign of Old Man Coleman this morning, although he usually waited till later in the day to check the neighborhood goings on. Even the basement—typically lit 24/7 in that dull, basement-lit way, which always stirred an uneasy feeling inside me—didn't appear to be occupied, although it was hard to see in the light of the rising sun. Dad said Mr. Coleman went batshit crazy years ago after both his parents, who had originally owned the house, died.

All I knew was that Mr. Coleman, with his black, thick-rimmed glasses, gave us all the creeps.

"Don't be so impatient," I grumbled, dropping into the low, black pleather seat. I positioned my canvas tote on the floor between my Nike cross-trainers, rarely used for runs anymore, since I could barely get out bed. "Have you even considered that all the shoes stocked in that warehouse might be stolen and we're aiding and abetting criminals?" I clicked my seat belt and leaned my head against the headrest, attempting to catch a few more minutes of sleep.

How do I find out if the cashier's dead?

"Yeah, Janice mentioned that could be a possibility. But I'm not asking questions and neither should you, my friend," Frankie slid his black sunglasses down from the top of his gelled bed-head hair and put the car in reverse. "One more week of slave labor making twenty bucks an hour is a lot more than you're gonna make scooping ice cream before Holly the Hag closes for the season."

I didn't answer, my eyes still closed.

"So, did your dad stay over at his new chick's? No truck in the driveway, figured I could beep as loud as I wanted to get your ass out of bed." Frankie eyed me as he checked right, then left, and finally backed out from the low-slung rock wall lining my driveway. "BTW, you look like hell, or as my grandpa used to say, a pile of mashed potatoes."

"Awesome," I replied. "I thought best friends were supposed to support each other."

"I am supporting you," Frankie said, with one hand on the wheel, while Khalid played at a volume level of four in the background. "I'm the guy you can count on to tell you when you got spinach stuck in your teeth."

"No wonder that beach babe broke up with you after a week," I said, opening one eye and then closing it again, hoping Frankie wouldn't probe, hoping I wouldn't have to tell him about what I saw, affirming yet again I was the weird friend in the group.

"Ha ha ha, please, she couldn't handle this," Frankie scoffed, pointing his four fingers toward his wiry frame.

The gruesome scene replayed behind my eyes, causing me to gasp. I flung open my lids and gripped my sweatpants in the creased sections beside both knees.

"Dude, you okay?" Frankie asked, taking a turn along the back road.

A thought popped into my mind, like a parachute descending into my brain: maybe I should have called Dad and told him about my dream, or at least ask Tina if the cashier was okay. Dad never liked to hear about my dreams, though, his shoulder doing that rotating move whenever the subject came up. I blinked, causing the parachute in my mind to deflate.

"Did you have another nightmare?" Frankie asked, turning to me.

I bit the inside of my cheek, dark and light green trees blurring together on the side of Kingston Road. I needed to know whether Denise the cashier was alive. Maybe I'd get a sign, some cardinal flying randomly across the hood of the car or something, letting me know she was okay, or that I should find out for sure. I swallowed, hard. Was that even possible, that I actually saw something happen in real life? Could that be true?

"C'mon, give it up," Frankie demanded.

When I was eight, I saw my mother smile at me once, in that gossamer space before falling asleep. I told Dad and Avo one night at supper, all excited in that little kid kind of way, like when you say you saw the tooth fairy fly in your room and leave the dollar under your pillow. My grandmother had lovingly placed her hand, still bearing her wedding ring, on mine, after she had glanced over at my dad. She then told me it was my imagination playing tricks on me. I never said anything after that. Even then, I knew it wasn't my imagination, though I never again saw my mom's face.

I scrunched my toes in my sneakers, tightened my stomach. "You know that really nice but awkward cashier with the matted down hair at the Natural Grocer?"

"The one with the dark-rimmed glasses like Professor Trelawney in Harry Potter, who never looks you in the eye but says thank you a hundred times?" Frankie asked, adjusting his glasses on his face.

"Yeah, that one," I said. I chewed on my lip, a dirt smudge of someone else's sneaker imprinted on Frankie's glove compartment.

"Well?" Frankie asked. He looked over at me for a moment longer than he knew he should have, turning the wheel hard to avoid a mailbox he had driven too close to.

Marshmello and Khalid's song "Silence" faded on the radio, some commercial about kids being cast in a Disney movie taking its place.

"She was in my dream last night." I cracked the thumb of my left hand. "I watched her get attacked by this weird-looking guy with wild eyes, like someone who could really snap."

"Whoa, that's messed up," Frankie said, his eyes widening behind his sunglasses.

"Yeah," I said, trying to get my thumb to crack again. "I got the sense the guy who attacked her might also be her boyfriend. And also that she might be dead."

Frankie slowed the car, turned the radio down to a level of one. "Dude. Are you sure those cop shows on TV aren't messing with your sleep?"

I turned to Frankie, my eyes narrowed. "Have you met me? I don't watch those stupid shows. I have enough drama in my dreams."

Frankie skipped the highway ramp that we usually took to work. He drove past the self-service gas station in the adjacent town of Norris that was busy for a Sunday morning and instead pulled over into the empty parking lot of Not Your Average Joe's and put the car in park. "Hold on. Do we know if weird-but-nice girl's alive? She has to be alive. We would have heard if she wasn't, right? Your dad's banging the owner of the store."

I shot Frankie a look.

"Sorry, I'm just saying," Frankie said, holding his palms up in surrender. "Do you know if weird girl is dead or alive? I can't even believe I just said that sentence."

"No, I mean she probably is," I said, my stomach tying in knots, making me feel like I wanted to throw up, just hearing myself talk about the situation-that-wasn't-even-a-situation out loud. "It just seemed so real. Like it actually happened." I dug a fingernail into my arm.

Frankie scratched his head, his hair sticking up like twine and sticks out of a bird's nest.

"What do you wanna do? Don't you think we should just go there and find out so you can feel better?"

"I don't know," I said. I pinched the skin where I dug in my nail. "I don't know what to do. But I feel like I need to do something."

Frankie leaned on the wheel and glanced over at the clock. We were already late for our shift. "Did you tell your dad?"

I stared at a section of maple trees across the street, surrounding the Jackson Reservoir in Norris, dappling in the sunlight, half the leaves still shaded from the morning sun.

If you tricked your mind, you could look at one part of the tree and think it was eight at night instead of eight-thirty in the morning. "He stayed out last night. Besides, you know how he gets when I mention this stuff."

Frankie exhaled into his fist, the way you do when you warm your hands when it's cold.

"All right, there's only one way to find out. And that means we're not going to be unloading boxes today, my friend."

I stared down at my nails, nail-biting a habit I developed in third grade. "Frankie?"

Frankie paused before putting the car in drive.

"I know this might sound crazy," I said.

"Crazier than seeing someone dead?"

"It's more than me feeling like I have to do something." I slid my sneakers on the dusty floor mat. "It's almost like, like *somebody else* wants me to do something. As if there's some reason these things are happening to me."

Frankie chuckled, leaned toward my side of the car, and nudged my shoulder. I looked up, following the direction of his finger pointed toward the car antenna protruding from the windshield. "Check it out. It's one of your signs."

A dragonfly—the symbol Gram declared represented my mom in the spirit world, the 14K gold symbol she wore daily around her neck and then gifted to me on my thirteenth birthday—perched atop the silver antenna of Frankie's new but gently used Jetta, flapping its delicate royal-blue, papery wings.

CHAPTER EIGHT

Frankie turned the car around and drove back to Hanley, directly into the pothole-laden parking lot of the Natural Grocer. A few cars filled the twelve spaces in front of the store.

I glanced across Route 53, where Bill, one of Dad's long-time employees, in his grey Michelin sweatshirt and jeans, pumped gas into the side of a large white Suburban.

"What are you going to do when you see her?" Frankie asked, as he pulled into the second space from the entrance.

"I don't know," I said, biting on my fingernail. "What can I say—hey, I don't really know you well, but I had a dream that you might have died, so heads up?"

Frankie quickly checked his hair in the rearview mirror and grabbed cash out of the middle console. "There's no way this chick is dead. C'mon."

Flyers advertising upcoming Drum Circles on Columbus Day weekend, Kombuchas on Sale for $2.99, and Gluten- Free Bread for 20% off during the month of October decorated the storefront, covering most of the glass. Frankie stuffed the five-dollar bill into the pocket of his jeans and then held the door open for me under the dark green awning.

A burly woman in some Reggae festival sweatshirt with a yellow bandana wrapped around her head occupied the first of two registers on the grocery side of the store. What if Denise wasn't scheduled to work? How would I know if she was okay?

"Hi, Devon," the friendly, sweet female voice sounded vaguely familiar.

I turned from where I had been staring at the shelves of B-Fresh gum and Yummy Earth bags of lollipops that shielded the second, unoccupied register in the left-hand side of the store.

Tina, the auburn, curly-haired owner of the Natural Grocer, the one who had recently taken up with my father, stood in the aisle in front of me, beside the shelves lined with gluten-free granola bars and organic, cardboard-tasting potato chips. Smiling, her hazel eyes mascara-less, Tina chewed a piece gum— organic, no doubt.

I had only met Tina once, two weeks ago when Dad and I frequented her facility to purchase some probiotic concoction she suggested for Dad. Today, she sported a brown and green peasant shirt that slung off her shoulders, exposing a splatter of reddish-brown freckles.

Big hoop earrings hung low from her earlobes, as if they were trying too hard.

"Hi," I responded, with a closed smile. I twirled the dragonfly pendant that fell just past my collarbone between my fingers. Gwen said once that when I didn't like someone, it showed.

Not that I had anything against Tina. I didn't. She seemed perfectly nice—one of the better ones actually, and definitely a little more au natural. I just preferred not to come face-to-face with the woman I knew was sleeping with my father. Though I probably should have cut Tina some slack, since she had lasted longer than the others. Dad had been dating Tina for a couple of months.

"Your father's over in the pharmacy section," Tina said, bringing her slightly mottled hands with clear polish on her nails under her chin. "Can I help you find something?"

A cascade of green—the way hiking trails appeared in pictures of exotic places— appeared in my mind. I could tell Tina liked my dad. A lot.

"No thanks, my friend is just getting something," I gestured to Frankie, who crouched down in front of a variety of protein bars, acting like he was deciding what to purchase. I turned and glanced over my right shoulder to see who was working the sole register in the pharmacy side of the store, but a line of gym rats holding canisters of protein powder obscured my view.

"This must be Frankie from the neighborhood," Tina said, flashing a smile, teeth likely whitened from Tom's baking soda toothpaste, no fluoride, of course. "You two go way back, right?"

"Oh yeah, way back," Frankie answered as he stood, clutching a 15 gram protein Quest bar in his right hand. He placed it on the counter, and reached into his pocket to pay the heavy-set cashier.

"Well, Devon, it's nice to see you again," Tina said, stepping aside for an employee sporting a goatee, who rounded the corner wheeling a small stockroom cart past the two front registers. "I hope you catch your father before you leave." She smiled and then started down the gluten-free pasta aisle toward the stockroom at the back of the store. I noticed Tina's denim jeans fit snug, and that it worked, for someone her age.

"Your dad does all right," Frankie said, nodding in approval as Tina strode down the grey cement floor with a high-energy strut, epitomizing the energy of someone who got up every morning to exercise.

"Easy," I scoffed.

"Hey," Frankie said, jerking his chin toward the pharmacy register. "Looks like everything's okay."

I clenched my stomach and turned, Denise's mousy brown hair coming into view. With a flimsy wrist, she clawed at the coin section of the register in her oversized tan cardigan that covered a Goodwill-looking Guns and Roses T-shirt and returned the change, without looking up at the muscularly built female customer on the other side of the counter. Denise—the cashier I saw beaten with a hammer in a vision earlier that morning— was alive.

"We good?" Frankie asked, tearing back the white wrapper and biting into a corner of the protein bar. "Hey, this good-for-you bar ain't bad."

For some reason, I felt like I wanted to vomit, not because the cashier was okay, but because this weird, intruding thought came in my head—that this poor girl had no idea what could happen.

Was I crazy?

What was the purpose of the dream?

Dad trudged around the corner and approached the pharmacy register, placing a few orange-colored bottles of Now vitamins on the counter. Mala beads wound tight to Denise's wrist. I tried to remember whether she had worn beads in the dream, when her hands covered her face in terror. A terror I merely imagined?

Dad received his change, the cuff of Denise's sweater that could easily have been her father's falling almost to her fingernails. "Thanks, hon," Dad said, causing Denise, who was used to my father's now-daily visits to the store, to blush.

"What's up, PJ?" Frankie sauntered through the sensor separating the pharmacy area from the rest of the store.

"Hey, Frankie." Dad raised his chin, and glanced over to where I stood between the two sections of the store, stuffing his change in the pocket of his blue dockside work pants. "You guys decided to blow off work today and have some fun?"

I stepped closer to my father, standing in front of the grape-rimmed counter, wood panels running vertically underneath, all the way to the cement floor. The border of the Formica counter had snapped off in various places above the wood. Up close, Denise had a callous on the side of her middle finger, the way someone might when they're bearing down too hard with a pencil. "Something like that," I replied.

I could feel my face grow pale as I stared at Denise, said hello, and attempted to smile through pursed lips, to make some kind of connection. Denise lowered her head the way people with little self-esteem do, then raised her palm halfway in the air to return the gesture, before she turned her eyes away from me, as if she might be judged.

Frankie quickly made eye contact with me before he turned back to my father. "Can you take Devon home? She wasn't feeling too great. I should probably get into work though, good cash, you know?"

"Yeah, I got her," Dad said, after he snagged the green plastic bag filled with vitamins.

"Don't be mad," Frankie said under his breath, walking backward on his way out the door. "I gotta make some more money to buy those high-tops I want. Later, dude."

"It's all good," I whispered, not sure Frankie even heard me. I had no desire to go to work, to make more money, or to do much of anything anymore.

Dad held the door open for me on our way out of the store, Frankie's loud muffler, by personal preference, already chugging down Route 53. Dad's eyes searched back inside the store before he let go of the door, likely searching for another glimpse of Miss Tina.

Outside, I shaded my eyes from the brightening sun, rolling things over in my mind. The cashier was okay—socially awkward and kind of strange, but okay. My head began to tingle as I walked toward my father's truck, as if an electric cap was suddenly placed on top of my head.

Thoughts immediately entered my mind from somewhere else.

She's twenty-five years old, was a misfit in high school, one of the ones who got chosen last in gym.

I stopped in place on the blacktop, my forehead scrunched. Where were these thoughts coming from? And why did it matter now? Clearly, I just had a bad dream. Clearly, everything was okay. I shook my head like a dog who just had a bath and hoisted up into the passenger side of my father's F-150.

Dad stepped on the brake pedal and turned the key in the ignition. Except why didn't it still feel okay to me? I squinted, the tingling and electric feeling giving way to a heaviness in my head.

The truck engine revved. I squeezed my eyes hard, trying to block out the thoughts revving to the same aggressive, unforgiving rhythm in my mind. Dad backed out of the parking space, faced Alante's across Route 53, and waited for traffic to pass while I sat with my head pressed against the window, praying the thoughts would stop. Dad beeped the horn to acknowledge his employees across the street and waved as he pulled out onto the main strip and turned left, toward home, as if it was just a regular day in our lives.

CHAPTER NINE

After we arrived home, Dad set his Dunkin Donuts iced coffee on the island and stocked the newly purchased vitamins in the mostly empty pantry cabinet next to the stove. "It's not like you to skip work," he said, his back to me as he closed the cabinet, his right bicep flexed. "I thought maybe you'd be going out to the dirt pit behind the industrial park on a Sunday afternoon, like we used to when I was in high school."

Silent, I sat staring out the sliders with my elbows on the end of the kitchen table, my hands folded in front of my mouth. A grey and white sparrow pecked at remnants of seed on the faded back deck.

A welling of energy rose in my throat. I had a weird urge to tell Dad about my dream, and why I really went to the Natural

Grocer, even though I knew the whole thing would cause him angst.

Dad eyed me while he gulped down the remainder of his sixteen-ounce Caramel Mocha with extra sugar. I clenched my jaw, continuing to watch the sparrow, and an accompanying blue jay that landed on the ledge of the deck before flying off to the feeder. Styrofoam cup in hand, Dad strode over to the table and pulled out the corner chair. The wooden legs dragged across the tile floor.

"What's up?" Dad asked as he sat his thick frame down in the chair and moved closer to me, resting his drink atop the table. Lines framed Dad's face around his mouth and beside his dark eyes, which I only got to see clearly when he was up close.

My forehead pulsed, lack of sleep taking its toll on my brain. I cradled the left side of my head in my hand and felt the words blurt out of my mouth. "I had a bad dream about that cashier who waited on you today." I closed my eyes, avoiding my father's expression.

Dad shifted in his chair and then moved aside the basket of napkins Avo had arranged so neatly in the center of the table. "Denise at the Natural Grocer?"

"Yeah." The point of pressure in my forehead spread outward, across my face. "I saw something happen to her this morning. She got attacked, real bad, by her boyfriend or something."

Dad sat back, one leg extended under the table, the same way he dealt with employees who approached him for time off, as if he needed a moment to think about their request, semi-torturous for the person on the other side of the desk. "What are you talking about? That girl was just working the counter, totally fine—well, I don't know about totally fine, she's a sweetheart but she's a nervous wreck, and I really can't picture her having a boyfriend, one who's normal anyway—but she's alive, for Christ sake."

"I know. I know it sounds crazy," I said, my voice lowered. I covered my hands over my face. "I just can't get it out of my head. It was so real." I could still see the number twelve in my mind, stuck, as if someone had paused a video screen to that particular frame in the movie, unless at this point I was only imagining that it was there.

Dad rubbed his hands back and forth over his thighs and then leaned forward in his chair.

"You gotta let this go. These dreams, they just—I dunno, they make you anxious. Bad dreams are like that, I guess."

I kept my gaze on a tile containing three crumbs of something between my feet, likely crust from the pizza my dad ordered from Mamma Mia's Friday night, since Avo hadn't been here for a few days. My forehead pounded like a bass drum. Even though he didn't talk about it, I knew my father worried about me having anxiety like my mother.

"Look, I know it's hard for you to let things go," Dad said, as he got up and laid a sturdy hand on my back, rubbing it back and forth. He crouched down beside my chair.

"You're the kid who can't let the bird feeders go empty for more than a day, even though they're supposed to find their own food, you know."

I nodded a few times, my father's attempt to make light of things. "I know. Okay. I'll try to forget about it."

"That's my girl. Tough. A true Alante." Dad patted my back twice and stood, his knees making a cracking sound. *But I'm half Keneally, too,* I thought, staring at the salt shaker in the center of the table.

Dad chugged the remainder of his drink. Wiping his mouth with the sleeve of his black polo Alante's work shirt, he tossed the can in the garbage pail next to the fridge and then punched his left fist into his right hand, in an attempt to rally me. "C'mon now, you're a junior in high school! What I wouldn't give to go back to those days! You're supposed to have fun and not be thinking of this weird shit."

My cheeks flushed. I returned my gaze to the crumbs on the floor, feeling like such a loser.

"Listen, Tina had me buy some melatonin for you to try, cause I wasn't sure if that Calm stuff helped. Maybe you can take that tonight and get some sleep and everything will be back to normal."

My eyes still squinted from my headache. I didn't even know what normal was anymore.

"We'll watch Jimmy Fallon tonight and make it a good night, all right?" Dad said, as he headed down the front hallway and into the makeshift office across from the living room.

I pinched my forearm, knowing this time I broke the skin. What was wrong with me?

How could I have seen something so clearly and yet been wrong?

That night I gave in and took the melatonin when I went to bed, barely able to concentrate while Dad and I watched television, my father cracking up at the *Tonight Show* jokes, while my mind completely wandered, causing me to miss the funny parts.

Waiting for the melatonin to kick in, I reread my journal entries, beginning to wonder if all this stuff I experienced really was crazy, like disorder crazy—cause nothing I dreamed had come true—and if I might be missing out on my life as a teenager in high school, which I knew in theory was supposed to be fun, or at least looked like fun, when you saw everyone else's stupid social media posts, which only made me feel worse.

I twirled my pen in between my fingers, fraying the fleshy part of my thumb. I hadn't even heard from Gwen or Frankie the rest of the day.

Around midnight, I slid my journal back in the drawer, my body growing tired. Lying curled under my covers in my tank top and shorts, my thoughts drifted in and out of sleep. Wishing I could talk to Gwen, recalling memories of Gram and I making cookies after school, picturing my mother and what she might be like now, if she was still here—all sorts of memories and thoughts jumbled together in my mind.

At some point, like waves slowly retreating from shore, I fell into darkness, into a dream, my eyelids fluttering above my lashes. Around 3:30, my eyes gradually opened, a feeling of a gentle but firm energy nudging me awake, *to remember*. The number twelve again. That piece came first. Then, I remembered I had seen the little girl in the room again. Yes, I remembered vividly now, with an almost eerie clarity. The girl had worn a nightgown, the edges frilled. I saw it so clearly, that piece, though her face was still fuzzy. She sat in that same little room, similar to a basement. Yes, a basement for sure this time. The little girl was alone.

Suddenly, my breaths began to shorten. I knew the girl alone was about me feeling alone. I already knew this. Why did I need to see it again, in greater detail? For what reason? Why did someone want to do this to me? My head throbbed, a dull persistent ache. I couldn't wake Dad. I wouldn't.

Just then, I felt something move in my room. More like sway. An apparition? Lying on my side, I froze, the covers pulled to my neck. A force. *Guiding me.* Guiding me? Where did that thought come from? Was someone there? Was this real? Or was I imagining this like a truly crazy person?

I peered deeper into the darkness. What if the force, the presence, was negative, what Avo would refer to as evil spirits? Why couldn't I be normal like other kids my age?

Sweat poured out of me as I contemplated the changes between Gwen, Frankie, and me; Frankie's bonding with his new football friends, most of Gwen's time last summer spent touring colleges and with her boyfriend, and how alone I really did feel.

I closed my eyes, tight. Suddenly, I spiraled into another dream.

My mother appeared, standing a few feet back from a foggy window, more like a shadow of her, a silhouette, inside a Victorian, gothic-style home. Outside, I circled the window with the sleeve of my frilled nightgown, frantically attempting to clear the glass. When I finally created a little space with which to see, my mother, still in shadow form, mouthed the words, "I'm sorry."

That's when I lost my breath entirely. I sat up in bed, screaming with no sound, the excruciating sadness filling my chest at the thought of a little girl separated from her mother. Is that what my mother meant? Is that why she said sorry?

In the darkness, again I sensed movement. Mom? Squiggly lines filled the space beside my bed, creating an almost electric charge that I could see in the air. *Mom, is that you?* I clutched both sides of my head, wanting the thoughts to stop, all the questions I had to end, but not the connection, no, please, not the connection to my mother.

That's when the sounds erupted. A cacophony of sounds: choking, panting, gasping out of my mouth. The last time this happened to me, when I awoke from sleep fighting for air, I was in second grade. Avo had been staying with us while her floors got redone; she had come waddling in behind my father, carrying cool, soaked cloths in her hand to help calm me down in the middle of the night. Had I seen my mother then? Why didn't anyone in my family talk to me about these things?

I blinked, the hallway light bursting through the darkness like a silent explosion, causing the little lines of electricity to scurry out of sight. Dad hurriedly made his way into my room. He cursed in the dark as he fumbled with the lamp next to my bed. "What's wrong?"

The electric charge that had filled my room completely ceased. I had lost the connection to my mother. I murmured inaudible sounds, between trying to catch my breath, my back drenched in sweat.

"I can't understand you," Dad said, squatting down beside my bed, his eyes small.

My head pounded as if cymbals were crashing into the sides of my temples. "Are you having a panic attack?"

I've had so many panic attacks over the past few months, Dad. Where have you been?

My chest hurt so badly, my heart working so hard, too hard, that I thought I might be dying. I tried to catch my breath, tried to capture elusive sips of air between the clamping and potential shutting down of my heart.

"You're scaring the shit out of me," Dad said, his voice rising in volume. "You gotta talk to me, so I can help you."

I tried to speak between tempered breaths, my heart muscle locked tight.

"What the hell happened?" Dad asked, with a lump in his throat. "Did you have another bad dream?" Dad nudged beside me on the side of the bed, resuming his regular position on the periphery of my panicked world. It occurred to me then that Dad couldn't understand—what I saw, what I felt, what I experienced as a totally abnormal teenager. It was the same way I felt, always standing on the outskirts of the happy people in the world.

"I saw something, and I dreamed of that little girl again, in more detail this time," I answered, between pants.

"Whoa, whoa, whoa, slow down," Dad commanded. "What girl?"

"This little girl, I-I know it's about me," I said, my back heaving as I tried to slow down my speech, "I just don't know why it keeps happening, and then I saw something, something else."

Dad's eyes narrowed. "Like what?"

I dug my nails into my forearm. "I saw mom, in a dream, and then I felt like she was standing there, right there," I focused on the space where the squiggly lines had been, where I had sensed movement just moments ago. *Please don't leave.*

Dad stood up and ran a hand through his thick head of hair. "I think we gotta go to the hospital."

"What?" I asked, turning away from the empty space. I felt the warmth of trickles of blood on my arm from digging so hard. I wiped away some of the liquid, desperately trying to erase what I had done. "W-why?"

My father grabbed his chin, stared out the window over the driveway, morning slowly dawning. I remembered the time he stood in similar fashion once at Gram's house, after I had spoken with the school adjustment counselor in first grade, a year after mom died. The counselor, whose name I now forgot, had recommended I talk to someone outside of school, you know, like a real counselor, for people with problems.

Dad had put his foot down in Gram's house that day, spouting the words "not my kid," as he looked out through the kitchen window over the sink, toward Gram's neighbor's lot with the red barn in the back of their yard. Gram didn't agree and had tried to talk to Dad, but after she realized it was no use, she nodded, said she would respect his decision, and would talk with me on her own, which Dad seemed okay with. I remembered that conversation like it was yesterday. I had watched TV on the other side of the kitchen and ate cookies Gram made while sitting on my knees at the table the way I used to because I was small. Even while I watched the Disney Channel, I still heard parts of their conversation.

"Do you think there's something wrong with me?" I asked. I dug into my arm with my nail. The birds sounded outside, their morning schedule unaffected by my nightmares. "Is this what happened to Mom? Did she have panic attacks?"

Dad's shoulder twitched, while his hands gripped the windowsill. "I don't know what's wrong. I'm thinking maybe if we get you evaluated, they can give you something to stop the panic attacks, and all this stuff you're seeing, which is becoming a problem."

My father didn't believe me, never said one word about my seeing Mom. Did he think I made it up? I pulled at a section of my bedding. *I saw you, Mom. You were standing right there.* I sat up straighter, my heart racing to turn back time. "I only tried the melatonin once; maybe if I double the dose it might help?" Did my Dad, who avoided doctors like the plague, really want me to go to the hospital? Was I that bad? Drops of blood oozed out of the slits on my forearm.

"I think we might be past that," Dad said, turning toward me, his eyes red, tired from being woken from sleep. "Throw some new clothes on. Your shirt is soaked through. Then we'll go to the ER." Dad pushed away from the windowsill and left my bedroom, shutting the door behind him.

I sat frozen in my bed, split between wanting to yell at my father for treating me like I might be insane and wanting to find out if there was really something wrong with me. Did my mother ever get an evaluation? Was that the reason for all the hushed talk at family cookouts and dinners?

I pushed back the covers, my heart beating wildly inside my body. My legs wobbled as I pulled on a pair of blue, baggy sweatpants, holding onto my dresser against the wall for support. My eyes filled with tears, fogging my sight as I pulled my sweaty tank top over my head, tossed it on the floor and put on another plain white T-shirt, throwing a hoodie on over my shirt.

I was on my way to the hospital to be evaluated, at five o'clock in the morning, my junior year. I was officially a weirdo. There had to be something wrong with me.

CHAPTER TEN

Dad never turned on the radio to cease the silence in the car ride to the hospital. He stared straight ahead, as if beyond the highway we drove along, to some other place I didn't have access to.

I stared out the passenger window, the sky still dark, watching sparse traffic on the early morning commute, most of which led into Boston. I wiped back the tears that spilled down my cheeks, trying to make sense of what was happening. "Are you going to say anything or make me drive like this the whole way?"

"Okay, have you scratched yourself like that before?" Dad asked, his brow furrowed.

I looked at the blood beginning to congeal on my forearm, the sleeve rising up on my zip-up Gap hoodie. Is that why my father felt I needed to go to the hospital? Because lost in thoughts, I dug into my skin?

I pulled down the navy-blue sleeve. "You don't have to worry about me killing myself, if that's what's driving this whole thing." Floodlights from houses in neighborhoods behind the trees whizzed past as Dad drove sixty-five along the highway. Had I disappointed him? Did he consider me no longer strong because I had panic attacks? I bit my lip, experiencing that stuck feeling again between nervousness at the idea of that and anger that my dad still hadn't mentioned my seeing Mom. Did he not believe me? Or did he just not want to talk about her anymore, about what had happened, and how it affected our family?

"I never said I thought you were going to kill yourself," Dad responded, both hands gripped on the silver steering wheel. "I just—look, I know lately I've been out a lot. I just want to make sure everything's all right, okay?"

"You're always out," I said under my breath. A white car drove past my father's truck in the fast lane.

Approaching the exit to South Shore Hospital, I imagined my father turning the truckaround at the end of the ramp and going home, his way of telling me he understood and was sorry for all the things he couldn't say. Instead, Dad turned right at the ramp, the sky still grey overhead, and drove straight toward the cluster of hospital buildings at the top of the hill.

"I never said I was father of the year," Dad said, shifting in his seat before switching on the radio to the Boston sports station.

I stared out the closed car window, remembering how I used to feel on the ride to elementary school, when I just wanted to stay at home. My parents started going out in tenth grade at Hanley

High School. I know from the stories both my grandmothers told me that PJ Alante and Kathleen Keneally loved each other. "Crazy love" was how Gram had once defined their courtship. I hadn't had my first real boyfriend yet—going to the sophomore formal with Jake Carafella didn't count. Dad didn't allow me to date until I was seventeen, which I'd be turning December 20. I never really wanted to date anyone, anyway. No one interested me like that at school.

The only reason I went to prom with Jake was because I felt pressure to, since he asked. I didn't want to hurt his feelings. I also didn't want to be the loser who showed up alone. Jake played basketball and ranked in the popular category at school, which I realize is completely shallow, but it helped. It made me wonder, though, after that night, and our awkward kiss at the after-party at Gwen's house, what it would feel like to fall in love, like my parents had. Well, I guess at the beginning of their relationship, anyway.

After my parents got married at nineteen, right after high school, Mom had moved back home with Gram a couple times due to marital troubles. I picked up bits and pieces of their tumultuous relationship through gossip over the years at family gatherings. I even heard stuff at Frankie's house once, when Janice sat drinking wine with her girlfriends at the kitchen table.

Frankie's mom knew both my parents, having graduated Hanley High the same year.

During eighth grade, one night when I came out of the bathroom, I heard one of the women who sat at the table, with short dark hair and a V-cut sweater revealing her big chest, refer to my dad as a player, while she swirled the glass of red wine in her hand, silver bracelets dangling from her wrists. I didn't like what the lady said—and almost said something, though I wouldn't have disrespected Janice in her house—but even back then I knew the lady wasn't wrong.

The stereotypical high school couple—Dad played wide receiver on the football team, handsome with his smooth skin and charming ways, and my mother was his smart, blue-eyed blond cheerleader girlfriend. I liked hearing about my parents when they were young and in love. It sounded like their relationship had all the makings of a fairy tale, until my father cheated on my mother.

I never understood why my dad was unfaithful, when everything sounded so great. I asked Gram that once; her simple explanation being that my parents weren't equipped for real-life, long-term love. "They didn't have the kind of fabric," Gram said in her gentle voice. I had also asked my slender, dyed-strawberry-blond-haired grandmother, that same rainy day after school when we painted canvases together at the kitchen table, if she liked my father. Like, honestly liked him.

Quiet for a moment, the rain pelting the back stoop during that grey November afternoon, Gram, with her freckled hands from "too many years in the sun with no protection," moved her paintbrush in strokes that smeared light blue across the canvas. Then she said that she liked Dad "well enough," having known him since he attended the same middle school where I went to school at the time. After that she commented how pretty I had drawn a picture of the ocean on my own white canvas. Classy like that, my grandmother never put my father down, at least not in front of me.

Avo on the other hand, whom I knew loved my mother, often defended my father, stating once at one of the cookouts Uncle Rob organized every summer for Alante employees, that "a man's gonna do what a man's gonna do." Meanwhile, I knew that my Dad's dad, who died before I was born, had also cheated on Avo. My grandmother must have known what my mom felt. Whenever someone mentioned my mother's name, Avo wrung her thick, "made-for-cooking" hands and solemnly shook her dark, coarse head of hair. Sometimes, she'd stare at me when she came over to make supper, saunter over to the table and inform me that I had my mom's eyes when I smiled, even though the rest of me, she'd nod with pride, was Portuguese.

Hearing anything about my mom felt better than hearing nothing. Nobody spoke about her death, other than to say she suffered from anxiety and depression, drank to self-medicate, and that "it was an awful thing, what happened to Kathleen." As a result, Dad never wanted to hear about anything to do with the subject of mental health. Whenever someone like Gwen's mom, Kristina, mentioned that my seeing a counselor might be a good thing—especially after I used to ask to go home in the middle of the night during sleepovers when I was in elementary school—Dad would reply with his infamous line, "Not my kid."

No one argued with my father.

Not that I wanted a counselor or anything. I didn't. Though I did want someone to talk to about the dreams, and maybe my mother a little. I didn't bring up my mom much or ask many questions, because I didn't want to stress out my father. I knew he had to be hurting, too, in his own Peter Pan kind of way.

Driving into the hospital parking lot, the sun still not yet risen, I thought about how Gram must have struggled in her private moments with my mom's depression. Maybe she wondered at night whether she could have done something more, though she never spoke about those things with me. Gram was always optimistic during our times together, teaching me that life goes on and that our loved ones show us signs to let us know they're still here. She also taught me not to get frustrated with Avo or my father when they didn't embrace the signs like we did—Avo referring to them one Christmas as voodoo nonsense. Gram said that people give us different things in relationships—some are able to talk openly about tragedy, others choosing to tuck the memory away, unfolding the edges only on occasion.

That's what I missed most about not having Gram around anymore, I realized, as Dad pulled into a parking space in front of the emergency room entrance. I didn't miss my mother, really, because I didn't remember her much. When Gram died, though, a little over three years ago, I felt like the ground opened up and swallowed me whole. Gram represented the only person who helped me stay connected to my mother.

Dad parked the truck, then cleared his throat. "I don't want you suffering with these panic attacks anymore, or these random nightmares, or whatever the hell is going on. If I have to put you on medication to make this stuff stop, we will."

I stared at the cottage-styled building across the street with the pharmacy sign out front. With its thatched roof and stone walls, the building looked more like something you'd find in a fairy tale versus a place that sold medication to help you numb your mind. A few spaces away, a rail-thin guy and his tattooed girlfriend got out of a beat-up Corolla with a massive dent in the bumper. The idea of going on anti-anxiety medication or whatever they ended up putting me on embarrassed me. I bit down on my lip as I stared out the front windshield. I didn't want to tell Frankie or Gwen. Were there other options, though? Maybe medication would help. Maybe I wouldn't get these dreams anymore if I took something, these dreams that made no sense and didn't even turn out to be true.

I slumped against the seat, my eyes closed.

Dad jerked his shoulder. "Listen to me, I don't want you thinking you're damaged goods if you go on meds. You have panic attacks, that's all, and I want them to stop."

I stared at the dashboard, curling my toes into my flip-flops. "Did mom have panic attacks?"

Dad exhaled, his forehead and nose flushing red. When you witnessed the blood rush to my father's face, you knew he was bothered, since his skin was even thicker than mine. "This isn't the same thing. Your mom had anxiety on top of a drug and alcohol problem and it messed her up—that's all."

"But did she have panic attacks? I want to know if she did, if Mom had symptoms like this. You never talk about stuff, even about what I saw this morning."

"Do you like this?" Dad's eyes squinted, the same face he made when someone questioned him at work, like there might be a different way to do things. "Is this what you want night after night? It's 5:30 in the morning, for Christ's sake! I'd rather be home lifting weights in the basement with my music on, not taking my teenager to the hospital for a goddamn mental evaluation."

79

I felt like I'd been punched in the stomach. I curled my toes tighter into my flip-flops, wishing I could dig my nails into my arm. "I'm sorry if I'm a bother to you," I said, choking back my words. "I took the melatonin last night. I tried. And the dreams keep coming. I don't know what else to do. I can't just make them stop. " Dad still refused to address my seeing mom in my room. Did he think I made it up for attention? How could my father be so opposite from me in so many ways?

Dad rubbed his hand over his face. "Look, I just gotta make sure I'm doing everything I can. I don't want anyone to ever say I didn't."

I leaned my head against the back of the silver leather seat. "I want to understand things, too. I have to be okay. I'm an Alante, right?"

Dad grasped the door handle with his sturdy, former wide receiver hands, his grease-embedded nails below the tips of his fingers. "I'm trying to be the best father I can. It's not easy, okay? Let's let the doctors check you out and go from there." Dad opened the door, exhaled and stepped down from the truck. I couldn't tell if he exhaled from exhaustion or resignation. After a moment, I opened the passenger door and stepped down into the parking lot, wondering if I'd be getting back in the truck as a crazy person, or if they'd even let me go home. My head began to spin.

What if that happened, if I really was diagnosed as crazy? Was there ever a chance to become normal, like to learn how to be, or were you just one way for life?

I swallowed hard after I shut the door of the truck, my legs rooted to the ground.

Could you be normal at times if you were considered crazy? I wondered. *Was it possible to be both? Like, could you get through life that way? Who had the job of determining that?*

I sighed and followed Dad under the slowly dawning sky overhead, feeling dizzy and defeated. The double doors opened automatically when my father stepped up onto the sidewalk in front of the entrance, as if to say, *here she is . . . We've been waiting for you.*

In the distance, I heard the chirp of a cardinal. I couldn't find it when I turned to look, but I heard its familiar sound. Or did I imagine that, too? *Probably,* I told myself.

I stepped inside the emergency room. The doors closed behind us, sealing my fate. Guiltily, I told Gram in my mind that, even though it had come to this, I still believed.

CHAPTER ELEVEN

I stood next to Dad while he checked us in at the wide, circular front desk. My father's brow furrowed as he answered the white, pin-curled elderly lady's questions, never quite looking her in the eye. A dozen or so patients sat in the waiting area of the Emergency Room, a waft of cigarette smell hitting me hard as a woman in a cinnamon-colored sweater strolled past. A petite lady with stringy blond hair crouched over in her seat, while another older woman sat with her eyes closed, her face burnt brown like people who used tanning beds. A bloated businessman to her right texted while he waited for his name to be called. The couple I saw outside huddled in a corner by a table stacked with magazines strewn across the glass top.

Colors swirled through my mind as I pretended to be oblivious to everyone around me, yet curious as to why each of *them* waited to be seen. Food poisoning? Acid indigestion? Drug seeking? Those stories all over the news about doctors distributing meds like candy. Would that happen to me? Was that how Mom started? Did a doctor give her something for her mental anguish?

Once Dad completed the insurance paperwork, he surveyed the waiting room, his eyes small in that intimidating way he had, wanting, I knew, to sit as far away as possible from the crack addicts. With clenched fists, Dad led me to a pair of metal chairs in the corner of the waiting room positioned next to a tall, fake potted plant with rubbery leaves. He sat down, his shoulders tense, as if ready for a fight.

The puffy cushion made a hissing sound when I sat down in the empty chair. I recalled how Gram said in high school my father used to start fights with anyone who even looked in my mother's direction. My mom must have been his prized possession until they had me, and life got stressful. I guess my father wanted to continue partying—or "passing fancy," as Avo once called his philandering.

Ten minutes later, in her pink and green smock and leopard-printed clogs, Frankie's mom Janice spotted us as she wheeled a patient to the front desk to be released. Ever the professional, Janice finished up with her patient, crossed the room to Dad and me, and knelt down between our seats. "What's up?" she asked in her no-nonsense tone, more demanding than asking.

"Hey, Jan," Dad said quietly, his elbows on both thighs, lifting one arm to squeeze Janice's shoulder, since after all, Dad considered Janice almost like family. "Dev's really struggling.

She's not sleeping. Which means neither am I. Hoping we can get some medication to help."

Janice nodded. "Frankie said you've been having nightmares lately. Are you having panic attacks again?" I envisioned cigarette smoke coming out of Janice's mouth. Still a smoker from her high school days, Frankie's mom owned the fact that she set a bad example as both a mother and nurse, telling us time and time again, "Do as I say, not as I do."

"Kind of," I answered. Dad swiped at the end of his nose.

"Well," Janice said, tapping my knee, her warm, honey-brown eyes sharply contrasting with her harshly lined, weathered face from too much smoking, sun, and the elongated stress of an ex-husband who left to have another family when Frankie entered first grade. "At least you're in the right place. We'll get you something if you need it. As far as your dreams, I don't know what to tell you there, kiddo. Not my area of expertise."

"Yeah," Dad muttered under his breath. "Not mine, either."

Suddenly, several EMT's rushed into the front lobby, wheeling a gurney with blood splattered all over the white sheet that covered half the patient's body. "That's my cue," Janice said, as she rushed to join the whirlwind of activity that ensued as ER doctors and nurses surrounded the writhing male. One grey Adidas Yeezy sneaker stuck out from the bottom of the sheet, visible from the waiting area. I heard one of the EMT's report to a nurse with a clipboard something about a car accident in the town of Pemberton, the next town over from where we lived.

"That can't be good, huh?" Dad commented, as his cell phone buzzed. Reaching into the pocket of his black Windbreaker, my father held the phone out to view the caller, the word Alante's filling the top of the screen. "I gotta take this."

I nodded and watched the seriously wounded patient get whisked down the hall toward the elevator after a nurse in a blue coat, a few moments prior, had sternly called to her colleagues, "I have an MVA with multiple lacerations, possible fractures, and spleen situation."

I wondered if the patient's family had been contacted, since only the EMTs arrived before handing the guy over to the hospital staff. Once the patient headed upstairs, and some of the nurses returned behind the front desk, my thoughts returned to the potential side effects of sleep medication, or anti-anxiety medication, or whatever they might prescribe, and whether the meds might numb me out, or worse, speed me up. I hated the way I felt when I drank coffee the few times I had. What if the meds made me gain weight, like the pill did for some girls at school?

In the background, I heard half the conversation Dad uttered with Richie, the shop manager, as Dad pressed his mouth to the phone, keeping his voice low. "Shit, I think I just saw our driver. I'm at the hospital with Devon . . . nah, something she ate from the Fortune Cookie last night. Did you dispatch Hank? He'll figure out the safest way to tow it back to the shop." Pause. I clenched my jaw, hoping to hide the flare in my flushed cheeks. "Okay, good. I'll be in as soon as I can." Dad shut the phone off and stuffed it back in his pocket.

"What happened?" I asked, still wondering what else could go wrong from taking medication. What if the dreams really went away? What if my mother wanted to reach me again and she couldn't because the medication blocked my dreams completely? Wouldn't that be both bad and good? Acid formed in my throat.

"Bad wreck on the main strip in Pemberton," Dad said rubbing the palms of his hands over his eyes. "Guy hit a telephone pole head-on. Sounds like the driver was the patient those EMTs just brought in."

"I think it was," I said, looking over at Dad. "I heard one of the EMT's mention a car accident in Pemberton."

"Yep, that's gotta be it. Hank's about to tow the Prius back to the shop."

I froze in my seat, recalling one of my earlier dream entries. An image of a telephone and a red Prius flashed through my mind like a lightning bolt, the BC high school sticker on the back window. I swallowed and turned toward Dad. "What color car?"

"Red, a red 2014 Prius. Why?" Dad asked, before he let out a yawn.

Blood rushed to my cheeks flush, followed by a clamping sensation on my heart.

Did one of my dreams really happen?

"I-I was just wondering. Was it a teenager?" The words cracked out of my throat.

"Yeah. Apparently went to BC High—sticker on the back window," Dad said, shaking his head. "Kid probably headed early to school, texting like a friggin' dope."

The sticker. That was the same car I saw, the details too accurate to ignore. Dizzy, I gripped the edge of my seat. "Do you think they'll be okay?" I asked, trying to get the words out.

"How do I know? You saw the guy come in, same as I did," Dad sounded annoyed, tired. "He's gotta be banged up pretty bad. Richie said the car was totaled, but he's probably gonna be okay, paramedics got him out of the car." Dad rubbed his hand over his entire face, likely thinking about how he needed to get to work instead of being with me in the hospital to find out whether I required medication or not.

One of my dreams happened. In real life. I felt like I might faint. I pressed my feet into the floor and breathed out through my mouth, trying not to draw attention to myself. *I had a dream that actually happened.*

A moment later, a slender woman wearing a pink nurse's coat and shiny, black clogs called my name and then led Dad and me down the hall to one of the beds stationed behind a white, pink, and blue striped cloth curtain. The pretty forty-something-year-old nurse took my blood pressure and told me to sit tight for the doctor on duty, informing Dad and me how busy the morning had been, and how someone would see me shortly. I thanked the nurse before she left, though I hadn't listened to a word she said. I sat on the side of the sterile white bed and stared at the October calendar on the opposite wall, thinking about the amount of blood I saw on the sheet covering half that kid's stretcher.

I don't need medication, I thought to myself. *They might think I do. But I'm not taking it. Not now.*

Dad texted on his phone from a chair in the corner pushed against the wall, the seat my father always chose when out in public, giving him the option of not having to be part of a conversation he didn't want to have. I wondered if he texted Tina, letting her know where we were and that his only daughter might have emotional troubles. Or maybe, like he had told Richie, he might have simply said I got food poisoning.

I tried to calm my rapidly increasing pulse as I sat with my legs over the hard plastic rail at the bottom of the bed. I pushed my sleeves farther up my arm as sweat gathered in the crook of my elbows. Why would I have dreamed about that car accident before it happened? What if the doctor did diagnose me as crazy and tried to give me medication to stop the dreams, like Dad wanted? Should I tell Dad about the dream?

I opened my mouth to speak and a shudder ran through my body, causing me to nearly shut down. It reminded me of when too many cords are plugged into one outlet, causing the circuit breaker to blow. "Dad," I started to say. My father looked up from texting, raised his finger for me to wait, mumbling that he was in the middle of something. He never bothered to finish the conversation about the accident, or ask me how I might be feeling now that we were actually in a room waiting for the doctor to evaluate me. A minute later, a small hand fumbled with the curtain.

"I'm Dr. Breen," the wiry man greeted my father and me before he pulled the curtain all the way closed. "So you're having trouble with sleep?" The doctor pushed back the horn-rimmed glasses on his pointed nose with his middle finger and glanced at the grooves on my arm.

I felt as if I was standing inside a cloud, the energy around me thick, dense, rendering me unable to speak. I just wanted to disappear.

The dreams mean something. I wrote it down, what I saw. I can show you. Something's happening to me.

Dad stuffed his phone into the pocket of his grey, baggy sweatpants, leaned over his thighs and cleared his throat. "Yeah, my daughter is having a hell of a time. We're here to get something to help her sleep through the night."

"Well, that sounds scary," Dr. Breen said, wrinkling his nose as if something smelled funny. "Let's take a look."

Outside the curtain, I heard female staff talking about someone who needed stitches in room nine. I wanted to tell the doctor that I didn't need medication, I didn't need anything at all, except maybe someone to tell this to, but if I did tell the doctor—that the car accident victim the doctor's colleagues were treating at this very moment, I had seen crash into a telephone pole in a dream over the summer—would he admit me to the psych ward, because I saw things in my dreams, *in my mind?*

Sweat dripped down my back, the way droplets of rain spill slowly on windowpanes.

Dr. Breen made a note in his clipboard after eyeing me for a moment. "You're a junior, I see?"

I nodded, no words coming out of my mouth. I lightly kicked the end of the bed with my heel, attempting to act like I had it together.

"Yeah, she's a junior," Dad said, clasping his hands between his knees.

The doctor scratched another note across the yellow pad of paper, while he continued to direct questions my way. "Are you working?"

"Yeah," I said, a dazed look on my face, my body stuck inside some other space.

Dad leaned forward in his chair. "My daughter works at an ice cream shop a few days, and then at another job, a shoe warehouse. Sometimes she comes in to help me when my guys are on vacation. Doc, she needs her sleep to be able to go to work. And you know, school."

"Of course. I worked on an ice-cream truck at the beach during my summers in college. Hard to resist trying all the flavors," Dr. Breen joked.

I attempted a smile.

"How about friends?" Dr. Breen asked, peering over his dark glasses, black pen in hand. "You seem like the type who would have a lot of them."

I swallowed, trying to form the words. "I have a couple close friends, ones I've grown up with." I sat on my hands.

"Parties? Having fun your second to last year in high school?" It kind of annoyed me the way the doctor tried to relate, like he knew everything about teenagers. Had he ever dealt with a teenager like me?

Dad scooted forward in his chair. "She's kind of a loner. She hangs out with us—her family and friends. She's got a lot of acquaintances. Everyone knows Devon. Through my family's business, we both know a lot of people."

Dr. Breen scribbled additional notes with his black Bic pen. "Yes, well, it's still good to put yourself out there, part of healthy emotional development. So, tell me, Devon, do you feel depressed? You know what I mean by that, right? Lethargic, flat, unmotivated, those type of symptoms."

9 1

Was the doctor messing with me? Did he know I felt like this right now, not because I felt depressed, but because I couldn't explain what was happening, and what it meant, and that something I saw came true? "No. I mean, yeah, I understand. But no, I don't feel those symptoms."

I just want to go home.

"Ok, any feelings of wanting to hurt yourself or someone else?" Dr. Breen asked in a slightly higher tone.

"No." I answered, sliding my hand over my punctured forearm.

"Do you feel sad?" The doctor asked, scribbling words on the pad of notepaper.

"No." I shook my head. I felt my cheeks flush from lying. *Sometimes.*

Dad shifted in his chair. "She lost her mother when she was five."

The doctor looked up from the pad of paper positioned on his knees. "I'm sorry to hear that. How, may I ask?"

"Suicide by overdose." Dad spoke matter-of-factly, having uttered that sentence one too many times. His face though, eyes tired, lines around his mouth, depicted a different response.

The doctor observed me from behind his dark frames. "That's not easy—for either of you. How do you feel you're handling things these days?"

The baseboard heater hummed slightly in the corner of the room. "It happened when I was little, I didn't know her very long, if that makes sense." *I wish I knew her. I saw her though, in my dream this morning, and I felt her in my bedroom, but my father won't talk about it.*

Dad pushed back his chair, making a loud scuffing sound against the floor.

"That definitely makes sense," Dr. Breen said as he nodded his thin face. "How long have you had these dreams that keep waking you?" The doctor glanced up at the clock on the wall.

Dad's shoulder twitched. "Years. Bad dreams wake her up and she screams. They seem to be gettin' worse. At this point she needs something to help her relax and go to sleep and get the dreams to stop." Dad squeezed his hands between his knees, his knuckles thick, pointed in my direction like a weapon. I remembered the times Gram and I played the game "here's the church, here's the steeple," her hands soft, veiny, and fleshy, so different from Dad's hands.

I'm not taking medication.

"Sure," the middle-aged doctor nodded empathetically. "Medication is a possibility to help you relax a bit more at bedtime. I guess I'm just wondering if you've ever had someone to talk to about your nightmares, you know, to explore things a bit."

I lifted my gaze from the knee of my father's faded jeans. Was there really someone I could talk to about this? Who?

Dad squinted his eyes, as if he was staring into direct sunlight. "Look, I don't think my daughter needs someone to talk to; we don't really believe in that, in my family."

Dr. Breen itched at an area under his collarbone.

"Her mom had panic attacks," Dad continued, "and even though she drank a lot, and it was different, I think if you just prescribe her something, it'll help with all this—you know—craziness."

I rolled my bottom lip with my fingers and pinched.

"I understand your hereditary concerns, Mr. Alante. My thoughts, though, are more about giving you a resource referral for your daughter, in addition to prescribing medication." Dr. Breen smiled through closed lips and then turned back in my direction. "I do have to finish my assessment here, so I need to ask you young lady, do you have any drug or alcohol issues?"

Dad chuckled under his breath and his dark eyes glared at the doctor, the way he looked at people who tried to cross him, as if to say, *don't*.

"No," I answered, shaking my head. I fidgeted with the sleeve of my sweatshirt.

"Good," Dr. Breen said and tapped his pen for effect on the pad of paper, ignoring my father's glares in the corner of the room. "And how about grades? Do you have any idea where you might want to go to college?"

I pushed my hands farther into the notebook-white colored bedding underneath my hands, my thumbs digging down into the fabric. "My grades are okay. I'm not sure, yet, what I'm doing after I graduate next year. What were you saying about talking to someone about my dreams?"

Dad crossed his arms over his wide chest like a bodyguard in a nightclub. "My daughter'll likely work for our family business. As far as outside assistance, I don't think that's necessary."

Dr. Breen glanced down at his pager for a moment. Then, he asked me, "Regarding the nightmares, can you identify a theme? If so, it might be worth analyzing. I'm afraid due to time constraints, we won't be able to do that here, though I did love that stuff back in psychology."

I sat up straighter on the bed. "I don't know, I just see things that aren't, well, good most of the time. That's all." I felt my throat tighten.

"I tell her they're just stupid dreams," Dad said, his arms still crossed over his chest. "Sometimes I wake up in the middle of the night—I don't remember what the hell happened and I don't care. I haven't dreamed in years. My daughter, though, she can't get stuff out of her head. She's too sensitive. Takes on the world's problems." Dad scratched under his chin and added, "It was the hallucination, though, that she had of her mom this morning, that made me feel like we needed to come to the hospital, Doc. We gotta get something to make the hallucinations stop."

I felt as if some external layer of me fell to the floor like a sheet, exposing me naked.

Dr. Breen turned toward me, crossed one pencil-thin leg over the other. "You had a hallucination of your mother?"

I fought to keep my eyes from filling with tears. I just wanted to go home so I could reread my journal entries from the summer.

I glanced over at my father, his eyes small, his back pressed against the plastic chair that backed up to the wall. I gripped little sections of the sheets between my fingers, feeling Dr. Breen's inquisitive eyes on me, unsure whether the doctor's expression bore intrigue or concern that he might be facing a potentially crazy person.

"I don't know what defines a hallucination," I answered, releasing the bed covering. I lifted my eyes to meet the doctor's gaze. "I just know I saw my mother. I've seen her before, too, a long time ago, and no offense, Doctor, but I really don't want to talk about it with a doctor from the ER. My dreams aren't a problem for me. I know my dad doesn't want me to keep waking up, and I get that, but I feel like, well, like I want to know more about why they come to me. I feel like I'm supposed to do something with the information. If you think you know someone who could help me with that," I said, tilting my head, "Then, I'll take the referral."

A flash of anger crossed my father's face.

"Before I refer you," Dr. Breen said, silencing his pager, "Can you tell me the actual information that comes to you? Is someone telling you to do something? Do you hear a voice that tells you to do something?"

Dad shifted uncomfortably in his chair.

"No," I said, denying that voice I heard, aware that the doctor had complete control of whether or not to slap me with the label of crazy. "It's just a feeling of wanting to, I guess, do something with the information. Right now, I'd rather keep the content of my dreams to myself if you don't mind."

"Fair enough." Dr. Breen said, uncrossing his legs and then crossing his left leg over his right. "Do you think you're psychic?"

Suddenly, the room felt smaller. I felt air trap in my throat. I became hyper-aware of the stark-white walls, the little porous circles in the tiles that seemed to widen, threatening to swallow me whole.

Psychic? Gwen had used that term in the tree house after I told Frankie and Gwen about the vision of the cashier. Was I psychic? What did that even really mean?

Dad's phone buzzed in his back pocket. He glanced down to quickly read the text, then stuffed the phone back in his front pocket and scoffed, "Psychic? No. She's not some strange psychic. We don't have those kind of people in our family."

"It doesn't have to be something strange necessarily," Dr. Breen advised, his eyes peering into mine, as if I was a petri dish under a microscope. "I can't say for sure after one conversation, but my sense is that if this is something you feel strongly about, young lady, then I would pay attention to that."

I stared at Dr. Breen for a moment until he became a blurry version of himself. The only psychics I had ever seen were people on TV talk shows with hair that was too long and bore outdated bangs, and wore colorful shawls and clothing like they were gypsies traveling in a circus. Did they even qualify as legitimate psychics? Did they have to look like that?

"Last question," Dr. Breen said, lowering his head in an attempt to bring my attention back. "Are you feeling threatened in any way, from your dreams?"

"No." I shook my head. Did they mess with my sleep? Yes. But I didn't feel threatened. Not any more. And I didn't want to sit here any longer and figure out what might be wrong with me. I wanted to know what might be right with me.

Dad leaned forward on his elbows, jiggling his clasped hands the same way he did when he was trying to decide what to do when a former part-time gas station attendant stole cash from the register. "Like I said, I'm concerned about my kid not sleeping and about these panic attacks. I think panic attacks require medication, right, Doctor?"

"I understand your concerns, Mr. Alante," the nerdy doctor replied to my father with his thick chest and bulging forearms. "I agree with you, your daughter could likely use some much-needed sleep. We can't be sure it's the lack of sleep causing the panic attacks," Dr. Breen said, tapping his pen a couple of times against his chin, "but not getting enough sleep often exhibits in the form of anxiety. I obviously can't say whether this is what your wife experienced, but at this point, giving Devon some anti-anxiety medication to help her relax and not get so worked up about her dreams may be the best course of treatment, in addition, to possibly speaking to an outside counselor." Dr. Breen jotted a few additional notes on the yellow pad of paper.

I cracked my thumb with the four fingers of my left hand. Did they have counselors who specialized in dreams? Did they ever work with people like me? Would counselors even work with psychics, if that was what I really was?

Dr. Breen rose from his chair. "I'll jot down a counselor website for you to research. The site contains a list of practitioners and their specialties and the insurances they accept. You might want to search for someone who specializes in psychodynamic therapy, someone who works with the subconscious, which would involve dreams. In the meantime, I'm going to write a script for Ativan, so you'll have a resource to use in the middle of the night." The doctor retrieved a small, square script pad from the pocket of his lab coat. He scribbled on the top sheet and then the second, then tore off the two pages and handed them, out of respect, to my father.

"Thank you," Dad said. He stood and nodded once in approval, as if all was right with the world.

My cheeks burned the same way they did when stung by winter's cold. Ativan? I knew losers in school who sold Ativan to get high. No way. I wasn't taking any stupid anti-anxiety medication. I saw that car crash in my dream, and then I saw that kid get wheeled into the ER. That's all I needed to know.

"Devon," the doctor said, his hand on the edge of the curtain before he exited the room. "I want you to know, by my writing a script for medication, I'm not saying there's anything wrong with you. In fact, I find it quite interesting, something I would encourage you to talk more about." The doctor turned his bony shoulders toward Dad, who pushed his chair against the wall, like that was the right thing to do after getting what he wanted. "Mr. Alante, did your daughter have counseling of any kind early on?"

Dad looked confused for a moment, like he had been caught off guard. "She had an elementary school counselor she spoke to once when she started first grade, but I didn't want outside help. I got a strong mother, and Dev had her other grandmother then, too, and well, she has me. That's enough."

If you talked to me more, it might be enough, I thought. *About Mom. About what I see. Instead of dragging me here, more for yourself than for me.*

I decided not to tell my father about the car dream, knowing he might not believe me.

Now I don't care.

"Individual therapy or family therapy can be helpful at any age," Dr. Breen stated, holding the notepad against his bony thigh as the hospital intercom reported information overhead. "The main thing we need to deal with at present, though, is to get you sleeping better, young lady. I really need to get back to my rounds. Both of you, take care." Dr. Breen pushed back the cloth curtain and left it open halfway.

Dad twitched his shoulder, twice. "I don't need a shrink making me feel bad that I didn't take you to counseling after what happened." He stuffed the script for the anti-anxiety medication in his pocket, and then crumpled up the other small piece of paper containing the counselor website in his hand.

"Why'd you do that?" I asked, my eyes narrowed, as I pursued my father out into the hall.

"We got the medication," Dad said, before he tossed the crumpled paper in a trash barrel at the end of the hallway bordering the lobby. "You're my kid. Let's go."

CHAPTER TWELVE

I rested on the couch the remainder of Monday, taking a three-hour nap. When I woke, I heard Avo humming church hymns in the kitchen; Dad had returned to work. Curled up in the fetal position, I continued to flutter in and out of sleep until the sound of thick-soled shoes left the tiled kitchen floor, crossed onto the flat runner to the front hallway and pressed onto the medium-thick rug in the living room, causing me to fully awaken.

I rolled onto my side, facing the center of the living room. The hands of the clock displayed 11:30 on the small round table that also housed *Auto* magazine beside my father's chair. I wondered how many times Avo had checked on me while I slept.

"Hello, gorgeous," my grandmother said, in her husky tone. "I'm making chicken stock, one of your favorites." Avo wiped her hands on a dishrag and sat down on the end of the couch next to my feet. She set the towel in her lap, and tilted her L'Oreal-colored dark head of hair. "Did you sleep well?"

"Yeah," I replied with a yawn. Still cloudy and overcast outside, the dim room appeared more like suppertime than late morning.

"It's about time," Avo mumbled, rotating the long string of fake pearls she always wore around her neck. "Your father will be home soon. We'll have a nice supper. It's been too long. That might be part of the problem, your dad working so hard."

I stayed curled on my side, not feeling the need to respond. Avo wouldn't acknowledge that Dad went out as much as he worked. My father was both Avo's baby and favorite son. Even Uncle Rob knew that. No matter how many times Dad got into fights in his younger days, no matter how many times he lost his cool at the shop with customers who complained on occasion, my father could do no wrong in my grandmother's eyes.

"This anxiety thing," Avo said, as she picked up the dishtowel and folded it neatly in her lap. "You've got to get over it. Just go to sleep at night. That's the end of it."

I closed my eyes. If Dad was old school, Avo was the original little red schoolhouse. Things had to appear just so; church on weekends, bingo with her senior citizen friends a few times a week, hair done on Thursdays, family business held secret. My phone buzzed somewhere under the quilted blanket one of Avo's neighbors, in her own little house across town, had sewn for us years ago. "I'm trying," I said off-handedly.

"Trying's no good," Avo stated firmly, as she shook her stiff head of hair. "You either do it or you don't. Alante's don't have anxiety and these so-called panic attacks. I've been through the death of my brother, two miscarriages, and your grandfather's shenanigans, and I never once had a panic attack. I told your father that's what I was gonna tell you. You don't need any of that foolish medication. C'mon now."

I nodded while I felt for my phone under the covers. I knew my grandmother meant well. She continued to wring the dishrag in her hard-working hands and I knew, in that feeling sort of way, that my grandmother worried I'd end up like my mother.

"That's a good girl." Avo leaned over and kissed me on the forehead before she returned to the kitchen singing in a low tone, followed by the sounds of clanking pots and pans.

I rolled over on my side and turned on my phone. I planned to Google psychics and what a legitimate one looked like, versus the ones on low-quality talk shows and reality TV that made you question if the answers were staged. Frankie had texted twice from school and checked if I was still in the hospital. I knew it might be hard for Janice to keep that from Frankie, even with HIPAA regulations and all, so I outed myself, informing him on the drive home that I had a bad night, making light reference to the idea that my dad took me in for an evaluation just to be sure I wasn't mental. Gwen had texted too, from Spanish class after Frankie informed her of what happened, only after I gave him permission. After all, they were my best friends and, I suppose, had a right to know.

After I scrolled through dozens of websites listed as part of the 24/7 Psychic Hotline—grateful Avo couldn't see my phone as I viewed pictures of weird-looking psychics who offered readings for $5.00 a minute——my thoughts flew frantic inside me, like a fly trapped in a house that darts all over the place, seeking an open door.

I started a group text.

> **Hey. Back from the FF (that's Funny Farm in case you weren't familiar with that acronym).**

> **Frankie: Ha! What'd they say? They let you go home, so that's a good sign.**

> **Me: I guess. Gave me meds. I'm not taking them, though. If you guys want to come over after school you can, I'm just having supper with Avo and my dad later.**

> **Gwen: Sorry, just heard my phone in my backpack. I have to stay after for a tennis thing and then Andrew's picking me up (don't be mad). My mom's stopping by with food, though. She'll be there for both of us, k? What happened?? Did you have another nightmare? How come you don't want to take the meds?**

> **Me: I don't want them to numb me out or block the stuff I see. (Pause) My mom came to me in a dream. Then, I felt her after, standing in my room.**

I waited, unsure of their response, adrenalin surging through my veins, though I wasn't sure why; it's not like my friends ever judged me.

Frankie: ????? Were you scared? That's effed up, but in a good way, right?

Gwen: OMG. What did she look like? Are you sure you're okay? Now I really feel bad I'm not coming over.

Frankie: I feel like I wanna get out of Spanish right now and come over. Well, I always wanna get out of Spanish. You ok?

Me: yeah. Just trying to figure things out. It was hard to really see her in detail; the dream was fuzzy. It's hard to explain. I wanted to tell you guys something else. I had a dream that actually happened. There was a car crash in Pemberton early this morning, the kid came in the ER this morning while my dad and I were there. I dreamed about a car crash over the summer.

Frankie: How do you know it was the same accident?

Me: The dream showed me a kid in a red Prius, a BC High sticker on the back windshield. Alante's towed the car. It matched the dream I had.

Gwen: That's crazy!!!!

Frankie: That's effed up. Kid was probably texting when he crashed. I really gotta stop doing that.

I exhaled, feeling my shoulders release a gallon of tension I hadn't realized I'd been holding.

Gwen: This is so messed up, junior year, the most important year, and all this happening to you. Did they set you up with a counselor?

Frankie: Must have freaked PJ the F out. Did you tell him?

Me: About my mom, yeah. Not the accident.

Frankie: Smart. Boss man would probably be on your side about you not wanting to get your license. You'll be like those seventy-year-old ladies whose husbands drive them to bingo. And the hair salon.

Gwen: Yeah, with the white hair that looks blue. LOL.

I clicked over to Google while Gwen and Frankie bantered back and forth and searched a list of websites under "accurate psychic hotlines open 24/7." I cringed at the sight of the men and women with weird, uneven eyes, like either they were high or someone had cast a spell on them. Maybe that's what *they* did to their customers who called the number. I hoped that wasn't how the doctor pictured me, like just some lame telephone operator who got paid to talk to desperate people at all hours of the night.

I leaned up on my elbow against the scratchy couch, looking up the definition for psychic, which the Google dictionary stated as: someone claiming to have psychic powers, sensitive to forces beyond the physical world, a medium. I rotated my ankle until it cracked. Mediums spoke with dead people, didn't they? Was that the same thing as a psychic? The definition was followed by the words psycho, psychopathic, psychopath.

I glanced back at the group text.

Frankie: I wish I could come over, Dev, but I got practice. Gwen and I'll be there in spirit—get it? Funny? Not funny?

Gwen: You're an idiot.

Later that afternoon, I heard three delicate raps beside the screen door, the one Dad hadn't yet replaced with the storm window. Sometimes it would take my father until February, when the snow blew in the house, and he'd blame the weather.

"Hello?" Gwen's mom's sweet, gentle voice called from the front stoop.

"Hi, Kristina," I said. I hid my phone underneath the quilt Avo had placed over my feet while I slept. "C'mon in."

Avo scurried down the hall, the chicken-stock soaked dishrag hung over her rounded shoulder. "Hello?" Avo called, her brow furrowed when she realized she had left the main front door slightly ajar.

"Hello, Mrs. Alante," Kristina said, the white strap of her Lululemon tank top slightly revealed under her running jacket that slid down her toned shoulder. "I brought some macaroni and cheese that PJ and Devon can heat up whenever," Kristina said, with a wave of her hand after she handed Avo the container. "Whatever you're cooking smells wonderful."

"Thank you, dear. They love my chicken soup, so I made enough for days. Thank you, though, for your thoughtfulness." Avo glanced down at the glass dish. "Homemade?"

"Yes," Kristina said, her slender hands bearing two silver bracelets clasped under her chin. "The kind with the bread crumb topping."

"I think Devon prefers without, but we can always scrape off the top. Go on in and chat. My granddaughter's had a nice nap and is as good as new."

"Excellent. It's nice to see you, Mrs. Alante," Kristina said with a smile.

"Thank you, dear," Avo said as she observed Kristina's petite frame enter the living room. Humming another church hymn, Avo headed back to the kitchen in her size-14 Macy's grey and red print top, and black pants.

"Hi, honey," Kristina hugged me and sat down on the other end of the couch, her cropped, stylish black workout pants exposing her knobby knees.

"Sorry about that," I said, my hand to the side of my mouth, in an attempt to keep things light. "I actually don't mind crumb topping."

"Love her," Kristina said, with a dismissive wave of her hand. "I hope you're not mad that Gwen told me you went to the hospital." Gwen's mom had the most gracious manners of anyone I knew. Pretty, fashionable, and kind, I used to want her to be my mother when I met Gwen in first grade.

"Not at all," I replied, aware that Avo had stopped humming in the kitchen.

I turned on the television, landing on an episode of *SpongeBob*, the show Frankie, Gwen, and I used to watch after school. The clanking of pans resumed.

"Awww, I remember this show," Kristina said with a look of nostalgia on her face. "I wouldn't let you guys watch it at my house because I didn't like Nickelodeon, remember? So you guys would watch it at Janice's house." Kristina laughed.

I chuckled while I stared at the television and ran my thumb over the groove of my phone buried under the covers.

"How are you doing?" Kristina asked as she crossed one leg over the other and folded her hands in the crease of her legs.

"I'm fine," I replied.

"Good," Kristina said. "Gwen felt bad she couldn't be here. She had a tennis fundraiser meeting and then I guess she had plans with Andrew."

I chewed on my bottom lip as I continued to stare at the television.

"Speaking of," Kristina said, while she tucked her hair behind her ear, "I also wanted to ask you about Gwen. I'm not asking you to betray her confidence or anything, but do you know if things are like, more serious then Gwen's letting on?"

I shrugged and yawned, realizing how much sleep I required to return my body to a balanced state. "I don't know. Sorry, I'm just exhausted after everything."

On the television, SpongeBob erupted in some rant about pizza as he held a pizza box in his hands. I sunk into the couch and rubbed my thumb over the tiny grooves in my dragonfly necklace.

Kristina rotated her wedding rings on her left hand. "I don't know if you know this, but I have a sign for my mother, too, the way your Gram taught you about the dragonflies."

I turned away from the noise and flicker from the television, toward the pear-shaped diamond on Kristina's hand.

"After my mother passed, I found a shiny dime on the ground. My mom had always taught us that whenever a person found a shiny dime in their travels—it had to be shiny, my family liked finer things—that was our ancestors' way of saying hello from the other side."

"Really?" I cracked my pointy finger.

"Yup. Every time I see one, I know it's my mom, telling me she loves me," Kristina explained in her soothing voice, reminding me of the way water sounds when you're drawing a bath. "I just want you to know that I believe in those things, too."

I stared back at Kristina's sincere gaze. Then, in a low voice, so Avo wouldn't hear I said, "I don't know if Gwen told you the details of why my dad brought me to the hospital—but I saw my mother this morning and not only that, but one of my dreams happened, in real life. I didn't tell my dad about that, but I know I don't need the medication he wants me to take. I need to find someone to help me figure things out, like why this stuff keeps happening to me."

Kristina paused for a moment. "Gwen did tell me, about both. Honestly, I think it's amazing. What did the doctor say? Did you share what you saw? Did they recommend someone for you to talk to?"

I flicked my ankle back and forth. "I didn't get into the details. The doctor recommended talking to a counselor, to analyze the dreams further, I guess, but my dad threw the referral list in the trash as soon as the doctor left the room."

"Right," Kristina said, pursing her lips. "Well, you are old enough to decide if you want to talk to someone, Devon. If that's the path you want to take. I think you do need someone or something to support you, what you're dealing with right now, seeing all these things. It sounds like a lot. Plus the fact that you're not getting the sleep you need."

Avo cleared her throat in the other room, causing me to lower my voice almost to a whisper. "I don't really think I want to talk to a counselor. I'm not sure that's my thing."

Kristina leaned forward. "Tell me about your mother. I'm so interested that you saw her in a dream."

I turned up the television louder, careful not to have Avo hear. I know my grandmother didn't approve of dream speak, even though I knew she believed in angels and the afterlife and all things Catholic. She just didn't seem to believe in the things I saw in my dreams. "It appeared kinda far away, like behind a pane of glass. I couldn't get to her, which I guess makes sense now that I'm talking out loud. But I saw her." My throat tightened. "She said she was sorry."

"Oh, honey," Kristina placed her hand on mine. Instantly, tears welled in my eyes. I blinked to clear my vision. "That's really something. To have seen that, to hear her say that to you."

I felt a weird sensation in my stomach, an excitement almost, even as I felt sadness at having the opportunity to share my feelings. "I'm not sure what she meant, though, like what she said sorry for. I don't know if she meant sorry for killing herself or if it was about something else."

"What else would she be sorry for?" Kristina asked, clasping both elbows as she leaned forward on her legs, her bracelets making a clinking sound as they touched.

"I don't know," I said. I clenched my jaw, experiencing that feeling when I couldn't explain things, yet sensed something, knew something inside myself, even when I couldn't articulate it to someone else. I needed to find someone who could help me in that way, who spoke that language, a language I still didn't understand.

Right after that thought, an urging rose up inside me, stuck in my throat—like a force in search of an answer. Was I supposed to speak to a counselor? Should I go behind my father's back? Or was there another way? I felt compelled to talk more, to release the stuck feeling, like something else had control over my body, as if someone wanted me to keep speaking. "After, when I woke up," I continued, keeping my voice to a whisper, "I felt my mom in the room, like not in my dream anymore, but outside of it. I felt her, in real life. I—I didn't see her, but I felt like she was there with me. Does that even make sense?" I looked up, searching Kristina's eyes for the answer I needed. "Do you believe that could happen?"

Kristina, with her beautiful, makeup-less face, sat silent for a moment, hanging on every word I said. Then, "Yes, I believe that could happen."

I moved my feet like windshield wipers on the loopy blue rug that used to remind me of an anemone in an aquarium when I was little. "The doctor also asked if I was psychic, which I really don't know much about, or what that really means, other than the freaks I'm finding on the Internet."

Kristina smiled with closed lips. Then, "You have a beautiful sense of intuition. I've said for years to Gwen that I think you have something, something special. It's fascinating to me. I know your dad's not thrilled about it—he's not that kind of person. I'm sure he felt awful taking you to the hospital this morning, the same way I did when I had to take Olivia in for her eating disorder. I want you to know, though, that while I'm sure you're struggling with not sleeping, and with the things you're seeing, it sounds to me like you could be psychic. Which means you probably need to connect with people who see things and feel things the way you do."

"But who? I don't know anyone like me," I said, praying to God that Avo couldn't hear. "Every psychic I've Googled so far looks like if Ozzy Osbourne and Niki Minaj had a baby."

Kristina laughed and then whispered, "You can't trust everything you find on the Internet. What would you think about attending a psychic fair? The place where I take yoga is having something next week. Hold on. I think I threw the flyer in my purse." Kristina dug into the bottom of her brown Louis Vuitton bag propped up against the bottom of the couch. "Yup. Here."

I took the purple flyer from Kristina's hands and unfolded its several creases, ironing it out straight on my thigh. Angels Loft Psychic Fair: Workshops, Readings, and Vendor Wares. Check out www.angelsloft.org the bold lettering read.

"It's a great little place. Maybe you'd want to participate," Kristina said as she snapped the top of her purse. "But don't tell your father or he'll have my head."

Water ran from the spigot in the kitchen sink. "Don't potheads and people who believe in witches attend psychic fairs?

Do you really think that's me? I don't see myself like that, like those people."

Kristina laughed. "Those people go to my yoga class. I wish I was one of them! They don't have to look like the people you've likely seen on TV or the Internet. Sure, there are some people who might be a little out there, but who cares? Why not find out if you do have psychic ability? What do you have to lose?"

I rolled my bottom lip while Avo hummed loudly in the kitchen above the annoying chatter of Patrick Star on the television screen. I wondered how I'd get there, what kind of people might be in attendance, and how I'd keep it from my father.

"Maybe you'll check it out," Kristina said before tapping my thigh. "In the meantime, if you think there's anything I need to know about Gwen and Andrew and their relationship, well, I'd really appreciate the heads-up. And so would her father."

"What do you mean? What exactly are you asking?" I asked. I tugged on the end of my sweatshirt.

Kristina slid her ankles to one side, the way classy people do when they have their pictures taken. "This is Gwen's first real boyfriend. I know she likes Andrew a lot. She spends most of her time with him these days, as I'm sure you're well aware. I just want to know if she's in over her head, if things are a bit too serious. Between you, me, and these walls, her father and I aren't really fans of Andrew. I want to make sure I'm on top of things, you know, like I wasn't in the beginning with Livvy." Kristina exhaled, blowing out of her mouth the way you'd make a wish on a dandelion.

"Did Andrew say or do something to make you feel that way?" *Other than just strutting around like he's the hottest thing going?* I thought to myself.

"You sound like a detective," Kristina said with a laugh.

"No, not necessarily. It's just his eyes. He never looks Doug and I in the eye. To me, that says he has something to hide or that he's just not an honest person."

"Yeah," I nodded, recalling how Andrew looked at everything but my face the last time he visited Holly's when Gwen and I worked. "You're right, he doesn't look you in the eye." Different than the way Denise the cashier avoided eye contact. It was like Denise couldn't look you in the eye because she was too nervous. Andrew didn't look you in the eye on purpose. A choice.

A dark maroon color formed in my mind at the feeling of Andrew. The color seeped to the ends of the screen in my brain, like blood.

"I don't know," Kristina said. She pulled the top of her fashionable black jacket tighter over both shoulders, bringing me back to the conversation. "Maybe I'm overreacting, I just thought you might know if Gwen was in too deep, and if I had something to worry about, since she really doesn't talk to me as much as she used to. Which I suppose is part of being a teenager."

I clutched the edges of the stiff flyer in my hand, grateful that someone I trusted, the way I trusted Kristina, had given me a resource, even if I didn't have a clue how it would turn out or if I'd even end up going to the fair. "I don't think you have anything to worry about at the moment," I responded to Kristina's request. I figured that was the best way to answer without stating directly that I knew Gwen had thought about having sex after the sophomore dance but didn't go through with it, since she and Andrew had only been dating a month. Gwen had felt that was too soon, even though Andrew disagreed. At the moment, Gwen's business didn't rank high on my list of priorities, but even if it did, I wouldn't have shared Gwen's secrets with her mother.

"Okay, then," Kristina said. She clapped her hands together. "That makes me feel better. You won't tell I asked, right? I've been kind of worried sick. That boy just rubs me the wrong way, but if I say anything, she'll sneak behind my back. Then I'll be completely out of the know."

"Likely," I said, with a half-hearted smile. Kristina sighed before she zipped her purse. "Gwen's strong," I said, sensing Kristina's lingering concerns. "She doesn't put up with crap, from Frankie or me or anybody else, even though I do think she's a little too gaga over Andrew, for my liking anyway, but you know what I mean."

"Yes, I know what you mean," Kristina said as she gripped the leather handles of her purse. "Gwen takes after her father, as you take after yours, my dear, in certain ways. Strong. Competent. No one messes with you. Take that as a compliment."

"Thanks," I closed my eyes for a moment. "I will." In some ways, I guess I was like my dad, who he wanted me to be, at least. Lately, though, it felt in more ways like we were different.

Kristina stood to leave. "You know, honey, I just want to tell you that even though your mother isn't with you, she's still around. Your grandmother taught you about the signs; all that was meant to help you embrace that truth. That's what I believe." Kristina reached down and squeezed my arm, her fancy diamond ring sparkling on her left hand. I didn't want to raise my head, sensing I might cry. Too many thoughts filled my brain. Why wouldn't my own father choose to believe Mom was still around and that she appeared to me from the other side?

The teakettle whistled a high-pitched shrill. "Devon," Avo called from the kitchen, "I want you to get some more rest."

"I'll let you relax," Kristina winked and smiled. "I enjoyed our conversation." Zipping her running jacket closer to her collarbone, right before it met the top of her tank, she added, "Think about that event. It might be just what you need."

CHAPTER THIRTEEN

The following Saturday morning, I tugged on my black ankle socks while balancing on one foot at a time, careful not to make a sound in case Dad was still home.

I opened my bedroom door, dressed in my leggings and a long-sleeve, loose black shirt, the house quiet and still. Brushing my teeth in the bathroom, I prayed somebody would give me direction in my life today, telling me what to do about anything and everything.

The yellow sticky note on the fridge from Dad informed me we'd have supper with Avo around six, when we both got home from work. I made myself a cup of chamomile tea and poured it into the white Yeti mug Dad had gotten me for Christmas, grateful he'd already left so we didn't have to discuss the outcome of the Prius accident.

Once I found out a few days later that the boy—a kid named Sean Bishop, who apparently had been texting and driving—broke a few ribs and had nerve damage to his face but otherwise ended up okay, I didn't feel the need to talk to my father beyond our conversation the night we got home from the hospital. I had let my father fall asleep in his recliner that night, knowing where our conversation would end up if I brought up the car accident. I knew my father would continue to pass off the Prius dream as pure coincidence. That's why I also didn't tell him I registered for the 10:00 Developing Intuition, Part One class at the psychic fair on Saturday morning.

"You sure you don't want me to go with you in there?" Frankie asked when we pulled out of my driveway and then sped down Kingston Road toward the neighboring town of Norris.

"It's okay," I said. I stared out the passenger window, the houses blurring together into a panorama on the side of the road. "I feel like I have to check this out on my own."

I bit the side of my thumb, flashes of orange bursting through the blur of decorated October doorsteps. I hoped there'd be someone like me, maybe even my age, who I could connect with at the event. At the same time I prayed the two-day workshop wasn't an epic fail.

I told my dad I planned to help Frankie in the warehouse for an extra shift, not that Dad would have noticed, leaving for work earlier in the mornings after things had gotten back to normal. I had returned to school on Tuesday and, as far as my father knew, took the medication. What my father didn't know was that the orange pill bottle with the white plastic twist top that I kept in the bathroom medicine cabinet remained unopened.

"Hey," Frankie said. He ran his hand through his bushy head of hair. "You know I love driving you to work and being part of secret adventures—which, BTW, if you get caught, I will promptly deny any involvement with—but honestly, when are you going to Driver's Ed?"

I suppose the anxiety I felt about driving bordered on the ridiculous. I already knew the basics. Dad taught me first in the elementary school parking lot and then let me drive with him almost to the tip of Cape Cod, in the summer after eighth grade. It's just that was straight highway driving, at basically one speed, not operating the back roads with all their twists, stoplights, and turns.

One time, my head barely over the steering wheel because I hadn't yet reached my current height, Officer Will Mitchell drove into the Center Elementary School lot to have his lunch and caught Dad in the process of teaching me how to reverse. Officer Will gave Dad the eye, as if to say, "What are you doing, PJ?" Will's co-pilot, Officer Joe Mallard, who went to school with both my dad and Uncle Rob, patted Will on his blue chest, code for relax, eager beaver. The officers pulled alongside Dad's truck and chatted with him about business, ending the conversation by stating that they'd see him later that week when they brought their cruisers in for repair. Alante's Auto-Body and Towing handled all the maintenance work for the Hanley police.

"I don't know when I'll do Driver's Ed," I replied. I bounced my left leg against the pleather seat. "Maybe I'll take the course over Christmas break." Right now, I didn't want to talk about my anxiety over driving, or the fact that I wasn't on pace with what everyone else was doing. All I cared about was finding someone at the fair who could possibly help me make sense of the whole psychic thing, and how it applied to my painfully different-from-everyone-else-in-my-grade's life.

Frankie turned up the radio as he drove past the renovated farmhouses lined up on half-acre lots after we crossed the Hanley/Norris town line. Half-listening to the Drake song that played on the local hip-hop station, I started to count sixty-second increments in my mind, attempting to make the ten-minute drive go by faster.

"You sure you're good, going to this thing?" Frankie asked as he turned the corner by the baseball field in Norris, where Dad used to play on the summer all-star team in middle school. "I hope you're not going to come back chanting Om and all those weird sayings."

"I sure hope not," I replied. I stared out the window at the succession of red and orange maple trees lining the suburban back road. Half of me liked joking with Frankie; it brought me comfort as we drove closer toward something I knew nothing about. The other half wanted to shut the conversation down, knowing that my friends and my family didn't really understand.

We turned onto the main route, where the Eating Establishment—the local hangout Dad's employees frequented most mornings before work—sat situated on the corner beside a small red building occupied by a mom-and-pop travel agency. My father's voice echoed inside my mind, how he wanted me to be a normal teenager and have fun during high school, like he did.

A few yards ahead, past a tiny barbershop and Pepperidge Farm storefront, I spotted a blue-and-white trimmed sign bearing the words "The Angel Loft" on the left side of the road. A blue-and-white flag stood out front of the two-story glass building, which looked more like a law office or insurance company than a psychic place. Frankie pulled into the lot after a light-blue Jeep drove by in the opposite direction.

I felt a release of butterflies in my stomach. I carefully opened the passenger door of Frankie's Jetta—the blue Volvo station wagon next to us parked a little too close to the line—and set my sneakers down on the concrete. A middle-aged woman with a frosted blond updo and wearing different colored sheer scarves around her neck, stepped onto the sidewalk that led to the building, chanting verbiage I couldn't understand. A short, meek-looking guy who sported a receding hairline and wore an odd-shaped, dark green crystal pendant around his neck, kept pace beside the chanting lady, struggling to listen.

"Dude," Frankie said, adjusting the sunglasses on his face. "What's up with crystal guy and Lady Scarf?"

"Don't start," I whispered, not wanting to hear anything negative. At the same time, I hoped there were people at the fair closer to my age, or at least people like me.

The main conference-style room on the first floor of the glass building was lined with twenty-five card tables, organized for business owners promoting past-life regressions, homemade bags of granola, rainbow-colored chakra jewelry lines, and funky-colored meditation pillows. My face flushed, my feet glued to the lobby floor. So far, the fair appeared more like a farmer's market versus something spiritual.

I turned and looked over my shoulder through the glass windows, reconsidering my commitment. I heard the coughing, cloggy sound of Frankie's infamous muffler as he drove away, darting down route 53 toward some other destination. My body experienced a swirling, dizzying sensation, the same way I used to feel when Dad made me ride the teacups at the town carnival. Realizing Frankie had left and there was no way to reach him—he kept his phone in the glove compartment after being pulled over once—my heart dropped to my feet. I know I had told him to go but, like the way Gram used to wait to be sure I made it in okay when I'd walk into Center Elementary school after she dropped me off most mornings, I kind of hoped Frankie would hang around for a minute. Standing alone in the foyer, I told myself, *it's okay, I can do this. I want to do this.*

I pinched the skin on my upper arm, and watched a small crowd of people, a combination of middle-aged women and men—some dressed in colorful fanfare, others like they were about to plant in their gardens—browsing the showcased products and services in the conference area as the psychic fair got under way.

I stepped closer to the glass door, feeling young and out of place.

Maybe I'd text Gwen to come get me.

"Come on in," said a friendly, dreadlocked-haired woman dressed in purple leggings and a yellow yoga top as she walked past, barefoot, in the foyer. The wide-smiling woman carried two mugs of tea in each hand for a customer seated at the first vendor table in the conference room. "All are welcome," she added, raising one of the mugs.

I stopped in my tracks. Sketched in black, as if stitched on the side of the blue and yellow pottery-styled mug, with a swirled signature underneath that might as well have read *sent from Heaven*, appeared the image of a dragonfly.

I bit down on my bottom lip, took a deep breath, and then I walked across the foyer and entered the main room. A grey-haired woman in braids who looked to be in her mid-sixties manned a square card table like the ones Frankie, Gwen, and I used to crowd around when we sold lemonade in elementary school. A sign saying Tarot Card Readings sat on the table, typed in bold black lettering and encased in clear, cheap frames. The woman shuffled a dark-colored, freaky-looking set of cards portraying images of half-naked people and gnashing beasts between her wrinkled hands, while a line of people formed in front of her table. I figured they had to be brave to sign up for that. What if the lady predicted something bad?

I scuffed my foot against the Berber carpet, my eyes scanning the room, across random vendors: the mottled-faced woman wearing overalls who rubbed another lady's foot for a five-minute introductory session to reflexology—which made me think of Sal on *Impractical Jokers* using mayo instead of cream when he gave a guy a foot message for one of the dares; a middle-aged woman who shuffled an angel card deck that appeared far more inviting in my opinion, as far as readings went; and finally a bushy, red-bearded husband and kerchief-wearing wife who sold tomatoes from their local organic farm.

"Oh, excuse me," a woman said behind me, accidently poking my back with a large box she held in her hands. I turned, facing a fifty-something-year-old woman sporting a dark, short haircut with bangs that looked a tarantula's legs spread across her forehead. She must have noticed my lost-like-a-kid-in-a-department-store expression, blinking several times in a row as she asked, "May I help point you in the right direction?"

I cleared my throat, noticing the woman's fancily tied green-and-blue plaid scarf atop her thick, navy-blue sweater. "Um, yeah. I registered for the Intuitive Development class starting at 10:00." I felt stupid saying that sentence out loud, thinking of how my classmates would likely be spending their Saturday morning grabbing Starbucks and going to the gym for a mindless morning away from studying and SAT prep.

The woman blinked incessantly. She had bubble-green eyes that reminded me of Dory in *Finding Nemo*. I was assured that I made the right choice in telling Frankie not to come in with me. If he were here, he'd be making fun of everyone the entire time.

"Follow me. You're in my class," the woman instructed, jerking her head toward the back of the room, her mannerisms more like a real-estate agent showing a house rather than a teacher in charge of developing someone's intuition. I found myself a bit more at ease, excited that I might actually learn something I wanted to. "I'm Randi," she said.

I followed Randi, in her business-casual attire, through the swelling crowd in the main conference area over to a small hallway leading to several office-style rooms scattered at the rear of the building. It reminded me of the parish center at St. Bridget's, where the CCD classrooms were held, back when I used to go, before I made my First Communion. Maybe the class would have more people like me.

Framed words of inspiration like *Dream* and *Live Love Laugh* hung on the spongy, off- white hallway walls, making me think of the polar-opposite sign that hung in the mechanics' area at Alante's that read *Do Your Job*, Dad's tribute to Bill Belichick, head of the New England Patriots.

Randi opened one of the slightly ajar doors with the side of her tan, chino-style pants, still gripping the box. Eight chairs were arranged in a circle in the center of the room, occupied by four women and one man, ranging in age from early-thirties to seventy.

"Welcome everyone," Randi said in a let's-get-down-to-business manner as she set the corrugated box on the floor next to one of the empty chairs. "Thank you for registering for part one of the Developing Intuition Workshop, part two of which we will continue next Saturday morning."

I stepped inside the medium-sized room, noticing the black-and-white wall clock and beige radiator that ran along the bottom half of one side of the room. I stood for a moment, checking out the five adult participants in the circle, some with nose rings and shaved hair, weird, nervously darting eyes, and one with a strange crystal pendant around his skinny neck. I have never been one to look down on anyone or judge a person by appearances, but nobody in the room made me feel like I belonged. *Where were the people who looked like Kristina?*

I chewed on my lip, wondering how much of a moron I had to be to think I would have gotten something out of this. Did I honestly expect or even want direction from these people, who seemed nothing like me? These complete strangers could have been nutcases, for all I knew. *But I'm here*, I told myself. *I got a sign from Heaven. I have to take a chance.*

Never liking anybody to look my way, I clenched my stomach, as if I could retreat inside myself, while I made my way over to one of the empty chairs on the far side of the circle, in front of the beveled windows, without making eye contact. All the while I contemplated whether it was even possible to be both a regular person and a psychic at the same time.

Was I really one of these people?

Purposely choosing a chair unoccupied on either side, I sat down and slid my hands underneath my leggings and pressed my hands into the seat. I always preferred my own space. I didn't mean to be rude or anything—even after eleven years of school, when sitting next to kids I'd feel itchy and aggravated, wishing I could sit at a table on my own, without really knowing why, which also made me feel bad at the same time. I didn't want anyone to take it personally. Whenever I did get to sit alone, say if someone was absent at my table or sent to the principal or whatever, I always felt better, like a heavy weight that had pressed into me, suffocating me almost, disappeared.

I used to feel bad for the kids in elementary school who got in trouble for poking kids at their tables with pencils and stuff like that, thinking they probably felt like I did and didn't know what else to do. I wanted to push kids away who sat with me too, or at least tell them to be quiet, that they talked too loud for my liking, but I never said anything because I didn't want to hurt their feelings.

Instead, I imagined that if I ever became a teacher, I would have everybody sit in their own seats, with no tables or desks too close together, so that kids like me wouldn't feel weirder than they already did. I figured that sometimes certain kids just required their own space, the same way some adults just want to sit and read the Sunday paper in peace.

I crossed one leg over the other and flicked my ankle back and forth, like I'd drank ten cups of coffee—even though I didn't drink caffeine—taking in the roving eyes of the other participants, as Randi gathered packets out of the box on the floor by her chair. A freckle-faced woman sitting across from me, with feathered, auburn hair and knee-high boots—easily the most fashionable person on the group—reminded me of someone who'd have a cigarette sticking out of her mouth while she operated a jack hammer with ease. She sat back with confidence, her arm draped around the back of the adjacent chair, where an elderly woman with flat, short grey hair sat stony-faced, occasionally checking her plain, silver watch. A wafting smell of cigarette smoke, which I could never stomach, drifted in my direction.

"Let's get started," Randi said, setting the carefully counted stack of packets in the seat beside her and then clapping her small, manicured hands once for effect, prompting me to visualize Dory the fish flapping her fins. "I'm Randi Abelson, a local artist with gallery showings on a regular basis by day, and an intuitive and practicing psychic medium by both day and night."

Randi reached over and handed a stack of packets, along with a bunch of small pencils like the kind you see in bowling alleys, to the woman in a grey hoodie, who then passed the stack around to the rest of the circle, ending with me. I held my packet tight with both hands and pressed the soles of my sneakers into the floor as Randi continued. "I hold a meditation circle here at The Angel Loft once a month and give both group and private readings upon request. My schedule is booked out until January, so if you're interested, send me an email right away, my information is listed at the back of the packet. And please write your name on the white nametag in the packet and affix it to your chest, so we can all see who you are."

A few of the participants flipped to the back page of the slim handout, while I wrote my name as small as I could on the label so no one could really see it or call on me. I stuck the label to the left side of my chest and then held the packet down between my knees. I noticed the scent of clove, or some kind of earthy fragrance, not cologne, but more like herbs. All I could think of was how Frankie, before Tina took over the Natural Grocer, used to say the store smelled like Healthy Stink, which in a weird way, I totally understood. I tried to hold my breath without drawing attention to myself while looking down at the first page, *Identifying as an Intuitive.*

"Congratulate yourself for being here today, people," Randi declared, raising her chin, reminding me of a ringmaster at a circus. "It's exciting and both nerve-wracking to begin the journey as an intuitive."

I swiped my sneakers like windshield wipers onto the beige office carpet. *Intuitive.* A picture of a wisp of white cloud entered my mind when I rolled the word intuitive over inside myself, settling over me like a sheer, comfy sheet in summer. Every time I had thought of the word psychic over the past week, a deep, purple-blue color, akin to a bruise, appeared in the sight behind my eyes, evoking the strange and mysterious.

"Now, when you say psychic medium, what exactly do you mean?" asked Carol, a woman in her mid-forties sporting a chin-length bob cut, badly dyed blond to cover her natural dark hair. The way she pushed back horn-rimmed glasses on the bridge of her nose, Carol struck me as the kind of self-possessed person who didn't care what anyone else thought.

Shifting in my chair, I realized I was among a group of adults who were obviously looking to learn more about intuition, sure—and that was great and everything—but I didn't get the sense that anyone else sought direction about the rest of their life, the way I did, needing to know how intuition played a part in that roadmap, if at all. I got the feeling that some of the individuals in the room were looking to simply pass the time in their lives, bored at home.

I bit my nail, berating myself for not Googling classes for kids my age first, wondering if that kind of workshop even existed. I gathered my legs under my chair and exhaled the clove smell through my nose, attempting to expel the unwanted scent and quiet the noisy thoughts that ran loose in my brain.

"An intuitive is someone who has psychic abilities, who knows things about people, places, situations. A psychic medium, however, is someone who usually has those abilities, as well as the innate skill or training to communicate with those who have passed on," Randi explained as if she had given this definition a hundred times, sitting back in her chair with one leg crossed over the other.

"Like dead people, you mean," a sallow-faced man named Lawrence, who sported the crystal around his neck, commented in a meek tone. The brown cardigan he wore swallowed up most of his body.

"Like dead people," Randi responded matter-of-factly.

I cracked my knuckles and reached down to tie my sneakers, though they were already laced. I had never met a medium. I had an opportunity once, when Laurie Hanafin's mother—a girl from the newspaper club I had joined sophomore year to try to make my resume better, even though I hated writing articles—hosted a medium party last winter, but Avo saw the invitation and forbade me to go. I tied my shoelaces in a double knot. How could you trust that what a medium said was even real?

"I think I might be a medium, too, in addition to an intuitive," said Deidre, an androgynous-looking lady with her hair shaved on one side. She rolled up the sleeves of her grey hoodie and then coughed into her fist.

"Care to share, Deidre?" Randi asked, blinking a few times.

"People talk to me at night, in my dreams," Deidre continued, nodding like a bobble-head toy. "I can't hear what they're saying, but they're talking to me, which freaks me out when I get up to go to the bathroom. I need to know if what I'm hearing is real."

The hair on the back of my neck stood on end. I looked up, and after a few seconds, became aware of the fact I had stared at Deidre a little too long. She swiped sweat from one of her bushy eyebrows with her forearm.

"Yes, what is real and what isn't," Randi said, nodding her head, her one gold bangle bracelet dangling as she clasped one knee. "A valid question at the beginning of the journey. While we won't go into mediumship in this class—that's more of an advanced topic—we will talk about those freaked out feelings that often go along with being an intuitive. Believe you me, people, I understand. The goal today for you newcomers is that you'll learn some tools to leave with, to deal with your anxiety, and hopefully the motivation to learn more about intuition."

"Cool," Deidre said, wiping her upper lip that was dotted with facial hair with her sleeve; one of those people, Avo would say, who had no social graces in public. "I don't know if it's just what I'm seeing on television, like when I watch crime dramas. Maybe that's what I'm dreaming about. But I don't know."

"That happens to me, too," the auburn-haired lady named Debbie chuckled in a street-smart, straight-shooter kind of voice. She crossed her arms over her tight-fitted white tank top, displayed underneath a red plaid Duster sweater. "I think sometimes it's what we watch on television sometimes, playing out in our dreams, like if we watch a murder on television, then we'll dream about the murder, right, which can really make you think you're crazy."

My shoulders deflated. I knew that wasn't the case with me, because I didn't watch those shows to begin with—never needing to, because I had enough drama from my dreams. Did anyone here dream the same way I did?

"That certainly can be one explanation," Randi said, leaning into her Whole Foods Grocery tote, grabbing a bottle of Dasani and proceeding to take a sip. "But it doesn't mean you're crazy, which is what we'll be spending most of the time talking about this morning."

I heard the din from the conference area as I glanced back down at the first page of the handout. *Identifying as an Intuitive,* the title read, followed by three bullet points underneath: *No, You're not Crazy, Anxiety and Symptoms,* and *Self- Care: Protecting Your Field.*

My field? I pulled at the hem on my sleeve. I didn't want to talk about theories like we did in high school, and whether or not people thought they were crazy. I already knew I wasn't crazy after the Prius dream came true. Where was the content about what to do when you had a dream about someone else, someone who was real, and not on some stupid television drama?

"Ok," Randi said, banging her packet on her thighs for emphasis. She blinked once, hard. "Have any others ever questioned whether you're crazy?"

I closed my eyes, the hands of most of the participants rising in the circle. *I used to, up until last week,* I thought to myself, with no plans to share that information.

"Craaazy Carol," Carol said raising both hands in the air, one of them gripping the side of the handout. "That's what my husband calls me about all this psychic stuff. I don't care. I've been listening to him say that for years."

"Honey, my husband still doesn't believe," Randi said, adjusting her wool scarf so that the knot fell to the center, "and I've been speaking to the dead for more than twenty years."

I stretched the sleeve of my shirt past my fingertips. Not what I signed up for; I couldn't bear listening to a bunch of women talking shit about their husbands all morning when all I wanted was to figure out what to do with my life. I prayed the my-husband's-worse-than-your-husband session wouldn't last and that we'd move on to learning something.

"The intuitive in you will bring out all kinds of those reactions from other people," Randi stated. "Left-brain types, I call them, the ones who don't get it. Now, having said that, some individuals do have mental and emotional challenges. I'm not saying they're crazy, but they might have real things to work through, and that may or may not be you. So I encourage people to see counselors to work through those things first, though most counselors aren't going to work with you on exploring and developing your intuition, which is why I teach this class. God knows, I wish I had me back when I started on this journey all those years ago."

I watched the eyes of the others in the room land on everyone else, wondering who among the circle might be certifiably crazy. Not wanting anyone to feel singled out, I focused on a spot on the worn Berber rug. I tried not to size up the other people in the room any more than I already had, which made me feel awful and judgmental and no better than Avo, who wouldn't even allow angel card readings to raise money at the church bazaar last November.

"Yeah," Deidre said, in a low voice that reminded me of Ralph Macchio from *The Karate Kid*, talking more to herself than anyone else in the room. She rotated her nose ring between her thumb and first finger. "I did see a counselor once who didn't get the intuitive part. That's why I signed up for this class. We do have anxiety in my family, though. Both sides actually. And I still live at home, at 31—yeah, yeah, I know, don't judge, I'm saving for an apartment—my point, though, is that it can be rough to be around the dysfunction, say if my old man forgets to take his medication."

I tapped my foot against the leg of the chair beside me. I sort of felt badly for Deidre who, in my opinion, seemed like she had some things to work through. Another part of me, though, admired her courage as I reminded myself that not even two weeks ago my father had an Ativan prescription filled for me.

"Well, Deidre, I'm glad you're here. Today we're going to discuss anxiety, an ever-popular topic for those who are intuitives. Being able to pick up on other people's energy—whether they're in your work setting, standing next to you, or standing center stage in a dream—can often be an anxiety-provoking process," Randi said, her face contorted in empathy like we were some therapy group. "And good for you that you tried counseling first. The fact that you didn't get what you needed causes me to believe you're in the right place."

I pictured Avo in my head, and what she would say and do if she were here, listening to people talk about their anxiety. I remembered once when a young mother had a complete meltdown at the dentist office because they turned her and her two little kids away because she was late, and how Avo had looked her up and down from the waiting area in disgust, later saying to me on the ride home that it wasn't "becoming to show your emotions in public."

"I hope we're in the right place, with the money we spent on the workshop," Elaine, a woman in her late-fifties, said in a gravelly voice out the side of her thin-lipped mouth. Debbie shot the woman a look.

"Continuing on with the anxiety of intuition and being able to pick up on people's energy, how many of you suffer from headaches, intense migraines or stomachaches, particularly when you're among large groups of people or even when you're around certain people?" Randi asked, nodding like a proud mother duck as she glanced around the room, though skipping Elaine, likely on purpose. Everyone raised their hands in the air, except me. Even Lawrence, the guy I had seen earlier in the parking lot with the crystal pendant around his neck, who hadn't raised his hand the first time. Reluctantly, I raised my hand just past my knee. "Conversely, how many of you feel a lot better when you're outside versus inside a building full of people, whether at school, at work, or the mall?"

I stared at Crazy Carol's 24 oz. Starbucks Latte, stashed by the leg of her chair, recalling how I usually felt irritable and spacey when Gwen and I shopped at the Braintree Plaza, but never knew why, preferring the outdoor stores of Derby Street in Hingham.

"You probably operate better away from crowds because you're intuitive, my friends, picking up on the vibes of those around you. Intuition is not knowing how you know something about another person or situation, but you just do—and when you're around a lot of people at one time, it can become too much. Today, we're going to learn some breathing techniques to help you with those anxious feelings." Randi spoke in the same tone our substitute Biology teacher Mrs. Bennington used in ninth grade when she read off the regular teacher's notes.

I bounced my leg against the seat. I didn't want to learn about breathing techniques. I wanted to just understand what this meant for my life. *It had to mean something.*

"I know things about my co-workers before they tell me," Crazy Carol said between sips of her coffee. "Like the time I knew this one lady's son got engaged even before she told us at work. I just had a feeling."

The big hand of the clock ticked quietly on the wall. I wanted someone to ask questions about bigger things, like bad things happening, or scared feelings, and what to do with those. I didn't have the guts to ask the questions I wanted to ask or share the stuff that happened to me. I didn't want to look like some stupid worried teenager, wondering what to do about the bad dreams I had, coming off like a little kid who's afraid of the dark.

Lawrence folded his hands, turned toward the beveled window, looking away from the other participants who continued sharing shallow stories about the times they knew things before others did. I couldn't tell whether he was bored or had something else on his mind. A pale green color, like detergent powder, clouded the sight behind my eyes. Instantly, I knew Lawrence required his own space, similar to the way I did. He was trying not to become aggravated by the surface chatter, as if he didn't have the energy.

"There's two sides to intuition, people," Randi stated when the group finished sharing their examples. "There's the fun kind, like knowing when someone got engaged, and the not-so-fun kind, like sensing when someone is sick." Randi glanced over at Lawrence, who had turned back to the group for a moment, met Randi's gaze, and then looked past her shoulder toward a bookcase in the corner of the room filled with book titles like *Acupuncture Heals All* and *Hands of Light*, as if he had been intruded by Randi's stare. "This is why it's crucial to practice good self-care, which is the next section for today's class."

I scooted to the end of my seat, holding my packet in my right hand. Was Lawrence sick? Did Randi know that ahead of time, or did she know by her own intuition? Either way, I didn't think it was fair to put the guy on the spot like that, since he seemed a bit uncomfortable—especially if he had some illness and didn't want anyone to know.

I attempted to make eye contact, to let him know silently that it would have bothered me too, but Lawrence, his eyes milky and meditative, never looked my way.

Randi went on to explain how each person has their own energy field, extending approximately two feet on either side, and that when an intuitive person stands near someone else's energy field, they often sense what is going on with that person on a subconscious level, picking up on someone's feelings of negativity, fear, sickness, or anger.

"Another person's field can skew our own," Randi continued, "confusing the energy of what is ours and what really might be someone else's. Have you ever been in a totally fine mood until you spent time in the presence of someone else and you just thought it was you?"

"You mean to tell me I've been picking up on everyone else's insanity all these years?" Carol asked, collapsing over on her legs like she was drunk.

The class laughed in unison.

"It's crucial to be aware of your own energy, people, knowing what is yours and what is not," Randi instructed, her large marble-sized eyes becoming even rounder as she spoke. I scratched back and forth at my upper arm, the way you would a mosquito bite. "When you understand that feeling what other people feel is a part of being intuitive, you learn to protect your own energy space and create boundaries from those who might not believe in your intuition or that this whole energy thing is real." Randi's eyes scanned the room and then landed on mine for more than the second she took to address the other faces in the group.

I looked over at Lawrence, who now looked back at me, both of us experiencing the minor psychic violation of Randi.

"How do we protect ourselves?" Deidre asked, her eyes squinting, the way a little kid looks at a board when they need glasses.

"Self-care, self-care, self-care," Randi said, her neck moving downward like a crank. "In order to protect your energy space and be in greater control of your feelings, it's important to step back, breathe, and get the perspective you need to take an energy break, being mindful of whose space you want to be around. That, and using an imagined telephone booth to keep people's energy in their own area, away from yours."

Randi glanced over at me a second time, before she proceeded to teach the class the Telephone Booth exercise as part of the self-care segment. I folded the left corner of the top of the packet into a triangle, attempting to ignore Randi's stares—and whatever point she was trying to make about my life—and the fact that I was still waiting to get something just for me, something from the workshop to tell me exactly what to do.

The heat kicked on, making a whirring sound against the wall. The only time I remembered practicing good self-care was when I used to go to Gram's after school and there'd be a cup of chamomile tea ready with honey next to a stack of coloring books on the table. Everything organized so I could chill out with a snack and watch TV and rest after the long day. It occurred to me now that maybe Gram understood that school might have been an overload for me, and that I desperately needed the mental break when I got home. Was that why Randi looked at me this time— because I didn't practice good self-care? How could I, when I kept waking up from scary dreams?

"In addition, when you can't easily get away from a person or situation, like when they're in your own family," Randi said with an exaggerated eye roll, to which Carol let out a loud laugh, "taking deep breaths to calm yourself helps. Like this—in through the nose, out through the mouth. We'll do a few exercises now to learn how to relax more efficiently, which actually will help you develop your abilities."

I shifted in my chair, finding it hard to sit still. I didn't know how I was going to sit through a bunch of breathing techniques, with people I didn't know, that was no doubt going to make everyone in the circle look ridiculous. I couldn't even do the meditation at the end of yoga in wellness class because Frankie used to keep one eye open and make everyone laugh. *Besides*, I thought, scratching at my arm, *how would breathing develop my intuition?*

Randi began the activity after everyone settled in a comfortable position in their chairs, with feet flat on the floor, and asked everyone to close their eyes. I waited a moment, then exhaled along with everyone else, resigning myself to sit through the rest of day one, only because I didn't want to leave the room and stick out more than I already felt I did, and well, because of the dragonfly.

That night, after Dad came home from work, Avo finished setting the table, pouring Pepsi into my tall frosted glass while Dad stood by the sink talking on the phone to Pete, his head mechanic. "Let's keep supper nice for your father," Avo said under her breath as she topped my glass off with foam. My thoughts remained on the workshop, which I hadn't disclosed to my family. "No dream talk or any of that nonsense."

I placed my cell phone on the back of the chair behind me, adhering to my grandmother's no-phone policy at the dinner table. Only after Frankie had texted to ask if my dad had questioned why I didn't look sweaty after supposedly working at the warehouse, and I replied that my father arrived home after me and wouldn't have noticed anyway because these days he was all things Tina. "It's not nonsense to me, Avo," I replied, which was the truth, even if I did think some of the Developing Intuition class might actually be what Avo considered strange.

I took a sip of my soda, recalling the telephone booth technique. I considered practicing on Avo and Dad too, but then I felt guilty, like I'd be betraying them or something by

142

putting them in an enclosed box inside my mind, even though the enclosure wasn't even real.

I watched Avo put one of the pans in the sink, feeling like I was having an imaginary conversation with myself. I wondered if the class was messing with my head, making me more confused instead of helping me figure things out. Suddenly, like a slide show on a projector, the image of the dragonfly sketch on the mug appeared in my mind.

Taking another sip of my drink, I decided I'd at least do the breathing techniques Randi taught us to use at bedtime to wind down from the day, to release others' energy that may have stuck to us, like a magnet. I figured at the very minimum, it might help quiet my racing mind. I hadn't dreamed all week, though I continued to sleep in fits and starts. That bothered me. If I was going to get up in the middle of the night, I reasoned with myself, I at least wanted to remember something, to feel like someone, or something, was still there.

Staring at the fresh stack of white dinner napkins in the napkin-holder, I considered that maybe that was the point. Maybe not dreaming was a good thing—somebody or something was giving me a break until I figured things out from attending both days of the workshop.

I bit at a hangnail on the side of my pinky finger. What if, though, at the other extreme, I never dreamed again, and this was some random phase I had gone through? What if I was entering a new phase that would pull me further away from knowing why this all happened in the first place, pull me further away from having another chance to connect with my mother?

Avo poured Dad's glass while he finished talking on the phone. "I love all of you, Devon Elise," my grandmother spoke to me in a quiet tone. "I just don't like that kind of talk at the dinner table. You've both had a long day, the work ethic of an Alante. C'mon now, eat nice and enjoy the soup." Avo returned the liter of Pepsi to the fridge, patting my father on the arm as she strode past.

While I opened my fancy paper napkin and placed it on my lap, a thought drifted down into my mind, like one of those little white feathers you sometimes see floating in the air, but don't know where they came from, I knew Avo dismissed my anxiety and my dreams—well, what she knew about my dreams from my dad, I wasn't sure—as a problem, something to be swept aside under the farthest part of the couch, the place you never take the time to vacuum. Had my grandmother done that to my mom, dismissed her depression and anxiety, causing my mother to feel alone?

Dad kissed the top of my head—causing me to snap out of my trance—and sat down for dinner. Avo nodded once, her instructions for "now we eat." I took a spoonful of the chicken soup, the thick, salty taste filling my mouth, which prevented me from having to engage in the small talk I detested, much to my family's dismay. Instead, I thought about Lawrence, the possibly sick guy in the workshop, and how he actually seemed nice, even though he looked, and dressed, a little weird.

Swirling the soup in the dull white ceramic bowl, I barely listened as Avo told a funny story about one of the old ladies who got caught cheating last Friday night at bingo. I asked myself, if I dreamed about the car accident and it came true, did that mean I really should do something about the cashier? What if I didn't say anything and something ended up happening, like it did to that kid? Would Randi, or one of those other people at the fair, really be able to help me, like tell me what to do if I asked? The spoon made a clanking noise against the side of the bowl. How do you open up and ask a question like that?

I continued to eat my supper, smiling as best as I could between bites of food, as if I fully heard every part of my grandmother's story. All the while, I thought about the workshop next week, and if I'd be able to build up the courage to ask the questions I had. At the same time, I pictured my mother sitting at this very table all those years ago. Hindsight's 20/20, I know, but from my perspective, obviously my mother was struggling. Did anyone know? Did anyone realize my mother may have needed to have been heard the way people in Randi's class opened up and listened to each other about questions they couldn't ask anyone else in their lives, the same way I felt about not being able to talk to my family? The Alantes always dealt with things by putting the serious stuff aside for a good time, never addressing what was really happening.

I slid one foot back under my seat, and then rested it on the rung of the chair. I'm sure every family wishes they knew then what they know now. I knew my grandmother loved me, her only grandchild, even though she refused to entertain my dreams. I also knew my grandmother loved my mother, and my parents being together, often referring to them, still, as the best-looking couple in town. I wondered, though, for the first time, as I stared at the salt shaker separated from the pepper shaker a few inches away, whether my mother felt like an outsider among the Alantes, too, while sitting at her own kitchen table. I also grew curious as to whether the way my dad and his family behaved—the way they ignored the important things—might actually have contributed to my mother's depression.

CHAPTER FOURTEEN

"Is that incense you're wearing?" Gwen asked, crinkling her nose as I got in her parents' Audi wagon at 9:30 the following Saturday morning, the final day of the workshop. Looking gorgeous as usual, Gwen's jet-black hair and red lipstick highlighted her creamy skin.

"Well, I'm not *wearing* incense," I replied, while I stuffed my maroon, zip-up American Eagle sweatshirt deeper into the tote bag between my feet. "I burned incense in my room. It's supposed to clear the space." I moved stuff around in my bag, anticipating Gwen's reaction.

"Like from evil spirits?" Gwen asked, her eyes widening for effect.

"Not evil spirits," I scoffed, as I buckled my seat belt. I felt somewhat embarrassed by the fact that I bought the incense on my way out of the workshop last week because I pitied the vendors with no customers. "More like negativity. You know, clearing stuff you don't want around you. Think of it as a space detox." I didn't feel like getting into it with Gwen about the whole energy field thing.

"Whoa, that sounds intense," Gwen said before turning out of my driveway.

"I guess." I reflected that I had slept a little better since I lit the lavender-infused incense a couple times over the past week before bed.

I took a bite of the chocolate and almond Kind bar I had grabbed for breakfast out of the box Dad had gotten from Tina, recalling how the tall female vendor with the wiry eyebrows and no makeup had instructed me to open a window after I lit the incense, set my intention to release the old and open to the new, and visualize stagnant energy leaving whatever space I chose to clear. I felt a little weird about the whole thing, but I wanted to see for myself if it worked.

I still hadn't really dreamed either, nothing that pertained to my life. Except one dream about Lawrence lying in a hospital bed with an IV dripping into his arm. I chalked that dream up to already having the idea in my head since Randi alluded his being sick last week. The only weird, potentially significant detail that stuck out to me was that Lawrence had his hand placed directly across from his heart, on the right side of his body, which made me want to find out if something had happened. After only having one dream all week, or one that I remembered anyway, I wondered if the incense, supposedly having the power to clear negativity, also had the power to clear away my dreams.

"They actually had some cool crystal jewelry on one of the tables last week," I heard myself say out loud, without considering an alternative, more peer-related conversation. "Small pieces, in different colors and funky shapes—not like the big honking piece the crystal guy, as Frankie called him, wore around his neck. You should come in when you pick me up and check 'em out. They'd look nice in the summer."

Gwen twirled her hair with her left hand, her elbow positioned on the ledge of the open driver's side window. "I'll pass on all things strange, no offense to the intuitive development workshop. I'm saving up for a pair of Frye boots, in black, since I already have them in brown. Hey, so about our plans tonight, Andrew asked me to go out to eat when we get out of work. He's gonna bring his very hot lacrosse friend Jared I told you about. What do you think? Cause *I'm* thinking it might do you some good after everything that's happened."

I stared out the window while I finished the okay granola bar, if you focused on the dark chocolate. "I think you're blowing off our plans to grab Panera after we get out of work," I said, part of me not really caring about going to eat after Gwen and I got out of work later that night. I had been in a routine of going to bed earlier and practicing the breathing exercise Randi taught us that involved visualizing a hand-held vacuum coming in through the top of your head and clearing out all the cobweb-like thoughts that built up in your mind throughout the course of the day. You were supposed to continue vacuuming out the rest of your body, after you finished going through your brain, finishing out through the soles of your feet, but I never got that far, because I always fell asleep. Without using the medication. I still woke up during the night, but not like before. I wished I could tell Dad, but I didn't want to have to come clean about the class.

While Gwen sang along to the new Ariana Grande song in the background, my thoughts circled inside the brown walnut swirl of the dashboard. If the breathing techniques had worked to help quell the anxiety I had at night about everything I kept locked in my mind—and the anxiety I had in keeping the workshop from my father, whom I had told this week that I was going in early with Gwen to work on organizing Holly's barn before our regular shift started—I wondered if Randi would be able to help me decide if I should tell the cashier about what I saw in my nightmare.

I blinked and then reached down and dug through my tote bag, pushing aside two cans of orange soda, making sure I had packed everything for work later. Curious, I wondered if Randi had dealt with anything like seeing an assault happen in a dream, and if my stuff was weirder than what some of the participants talked about last week. None of which seemed that serious in my opinion, simply stories of coincidence versus content that could truly affect someone else's life.

"So, are you in?" Gwen asked as she changed the station after the song ended.

I pushed the sleeves of my long-sleeve T-shirt back, considering that if I did go on the double date, I just might be able to get Gwen, and everyone else in the quest of making me like other kids my age, off my back. Besides, if Avo found the incense in my room and then told my Dad, that'd be a whole other thing, on top of the nightmares. "Sure, why not," I said with a feigned smile. I could hear my father's voice bouncing off the interiors of my mind, happy that I chose to do something normal, and more like everybody else, even though I wasn't entirely sure what I had agreed to.

"Fabulous," Gwen said, tapping the steering wheel in victory. "Okay, the plan is, Andrew and Jared are gonna stop by Holly's before they go to the gym. Then you can both check each other out. Even though I told you—Jared's already seen you on Instagram and totally wants in on the date."

"Reason number 101 why I hate social media," I said, crumpling the granola wrapper and shoving it down into my bag while Gwen turned onto Washington Street. "Stalkers."

Gwen pressed her lips together, evening out her freshly applied lip color. "Stop. Jared's not a stalker, my friend—he's a hot stalker. Almost as hot as Andrew," she squealed, shrugging her shoulders to her ears, the way Sharpay did in *High School Musical*, the way Gwen and I said we'd never, ever behave.

"Well then, why wouldn't I go?" I said with a sigh as the now-familiar Angel Loft sign came into view. The Psychic Fair flag out front, stuck in the grass on the side of the road, rippled in the unseasonably warm breeze.

"My mom said they have great yoga classes here," Gwen declared before she turned left into the sunny lot and parked out front of the glass entrance door. Then, pressing the button to open the sunroof, Gwen added, "Have fun so you're in a good mood to go tonight. I'll pick you up 12:00 sharp."

I gripped the door handle, exhaled and opened the passenger door, hopeful I'd work up the nerve to talk to someone today to get answers to my questions.

––––––––––––––

"Welcome back, everyone," Randi said, handing out the packets from last week, a different gold bangle hanging from her wrist, one her husband probably gave to her after some life event, like being married for twenty-five years. "I hope everyone had a good week and enjoyed the homework exercises."

Debbie, who had been leaning over both thighs, immediately raised her hand to speak. "I just want to say that last time you talked about being careful around certain people's energies that can bring you down. I thought about that a lot because my mom, here, lives with my drug addict brother."

"Well, we don't know that for sure," Elaine commented in her throaty, smoker's voice while she scratched under her chin.

My eyes darted back and forth between the mother and daughter, hoping to God that today's class wouldn't turn out to be like some reality-television show and a waste of my time.

"But we do know, Mom," Debbie sighed, puffing out her cheeks. Then she addressed the group. "I always know when my brother is using, it's a feeling I get, which I'm understanding now is my intuition. When I'm around my brother, I get irritable, which I know is his crappy, drug-addict vibe. Lots of stepping back, breathing, and taking good self-care here over the past week," Debbie said with an eye roll, the rest of the circle laughing and nodding in understanding. "My Mom, though, she's had a few dreams where she sees my brother doing drugs but doesn't want to believe it's real—you know, in real life, and what she might need to do about the information that's coming to her in the dreams."

My heart raced. Someone else had a real problem, with real people in their life. Elaine gazed at the floor, her face ashen and void of emotion.

"That is a great lead-in to the next section," Randi said, holding up her packet as if she was brilliant and turning to the next page where we left off, prompting us to do the same. *"Sensing Energy and the Levels of Intuition: Clairaudient, Clairsentient, and Clairvoyant.*

I bounced my foot, exposed in my cropped jeans, under the chair, eager to find out the type of intuition I had.

"Most of you will likely have experienced psychic activity on one of these levels," Randi continued, passing around the tiny pencils in the white box so we could take notes. "Today you will learn more about the method that comes most naturally to you, and then develop that channel. Some though, with particular abilities, have experienced all three levels."

I fidgeted with one of the wings on my necklace.

"Clairvoyant is the ability to see," Randi explained, running her finger along the word on her packet, "whether in dreams like Elaine's, or in your mind's eye. Meaning, you don't experience sight the same way I'm seeing you all now, but with your eyes closed, behind your eyes. In some cases, people can also 'see' on that level with their eyes open, if they're particularly skilled, and trusting, which we'll discuss later. Being clairvoyant can be either an innate ability or a skill that can be sharpened through meditation."

I cracked the knuckle on my thumb, thinking how I saw things in my dreams and also the way I saw colors in my mind, when I was awake. The colors, I knew, weren't something someone else could see—real only to me—but yet still existed, in a way I could never explain to another person.

"Next is clairsentient," Randi said, swiveling her neck left and right to address the circle, "which is the ability to hear things on another realm—again, not in the way you are hearing me in this moment. For example, has anyone ever heard their name called before they fall asleep or early morning before they wake up?"

Lawrence, who appeared weaker this week, raised his hand halfway in the air. I stared at the turquoise bracelet on his wrist, thinking about my dream he was in, and also about how I heard someone calling my name the morning I was supposed to take the SATs.

"That's Spirit, trying to get your attention," Randi stated, raising her finger in the air. "Best time to get us to listen is when we're coming out of sleep, to get us to acknowledge their presence, because we're usually too busy during the day working, going to school, and on our damn phones. Now, if you have heard your name called, you may want to develop that ability further in order to potentially hear streams of information, which is entirely possible for some psychic mediums. That's how things started for me, in case you were curious. I had asked my dreams, when I first started this journey, to tell me what to take out of my diet in order to lose weight and to develop my intuition. The following morning, I swear to you, I heard 'take out shellfish and milk'. There you go, people, haven't eaten them since, except maybe on special occasions, but you get the point."

"You asked your dreams a question?" Carol asked. Her forehead wrinkled like ridges in sand as she pushed her glasses back to their original position.

"Of course," Randi said with confidence. "Keeping a dream journal to record information that comes during the night helps to quickly retain the answer to your questions and is also a great tool for self-care, by the way. Dream journaling is quite therapeutic."

I doodled in the margins of my packet, toying with the idea of sharing with the group that Gram had given me a dream journal and that I'd been using it for years, but then I changed my mind.

"Ask and ye shall receive, people," Randi said. She fidgeted with her shawl to get it just right. "In my case, what I asked for arrived in clairaudient form. See? There are differing methods of how the information will come to you, and you need to be open to how that channel will appear, if you want to do this work."

My mouth suddenly went dry. Work? Like for a job? I couldn't imagine doing what Randi did, teaching classes or being someone who spoke with dead people. Is that what she meant?

"I think I'd crap my pants if I heard a voice calling my name," Deidre said, sitting back and crossing her arms over her chest.

My face flushed as my eyes bore into the white peeled letters of some company logo on Deidre's sweatshirt, the black fabric faded and worn.

"Not if it was one of your ancestors," Debbie chuckled, reaching down into her knapsack and grabbing at a handful of sunflower seeds. "Sometimes, I hear my aunt, who passed from breast cancer, and I don't even flinch. I know she's watching over me." Debbie shimmied the seeds in the palm of her hand before pouring a portion of them into her mouth.

"How do you really know, though?" Deidre asked, crossing her corduroy pants at the ankles.

"That's what I say," Elaine said out the side of her mouth. She looked in the opposite direction, her plain face weathered, her arms crossed over her chest.

Curling my black, Old Navy foamy flip-flops into the carpet, I waited for Debbie's response.

"I guess you don't know for sure, but it's just the way I feel. I can't prove it, but I know it's my aunt Marlene. I hear her voice. Plus, I always notice the clock, and it's around 2:22 and that was her birthday," Debbie said. She smiled before sliding the rest of the seeds in her mouth.

"I notice the clock at all different times, too, when I get up cause of menopause," Elaine said dryly. "I call that a coincidence."

Elaine reminded me of one of Dad's mechanics, Zizi, an old-timer who had been around since my grandfather opened the shop. Uncle Rob had tried to get Zizi, who used to run card games with my grandfather on the weekends, to stop swearing in the service station, to no avail. Zizi always waved his hand at Rob as if to blow him off, saying, "I knew you when you were crapping your pants. Come on now, let me get back to work."

Debbie ignored her mother, sitting back in her chair and rubbing at her face.

"Now, what you just described in the way you feel, is the last level of intuition," Randi said, reading from the packet.

"That's being clairsentient. Clairsentience is the most 'popular' sense of intuition, if I had to explain it that way. It's when you feel something without being able to explain why you feel that way. Think gut reaction. Most people experience this level of intuition to some degree, yes?"

Debbie nodded in agreement, not bothering to look over at her mother.

I pressed my heel against the leg of the chair. I had experienced all three levels of being intuitive.

"Do any of you have any questions so far?" Randi asked the class while smoothing a wrinkle in her pant leg.

I dug my fingernail into the side of my arm, wanting to raise my hand and ask what it really meant when you had experienced all three. And if it meant you could do something for a job, not what Randi did exactly, but something that made sense for me? Would you even need SATs for that? Wouldn't you have to study criminal justice in college? Was there such a thing as intuitive criminal justice?

I scratched at my arm in a circular motion through my shirt, waiting for someone else to speak, feeling a little stupid about the questions I wanted to ask, figuring someone might just think of me as a dumb teenager trying to get out of going to a four-year school, until Debbie raised her hand a second time. "Part of why we're here," Debbie explained, "is to help my mom have the courage to listen and believe in the content of her own dreams. Honestly, I just want her to confront my brother already and kick his ass out, but that's a different conversation for a different day. I also don't live with my brother like my mom does, and don't have the guilt. Mom doesn't believe in counseling, either, so

I'm hoping you can help her solve this problem, since she won't listen to me."

Stone-faced, Elaine stared at the floor, her arms crossed snug over her chest as if she was holding it together until she could go outside and have a cigarette.

"I think my mom questions the validity of her dreams," Debbie said, draping her arm around the back of Elaine's chair. "Like how is it possible that she's being shown this stuff, in an am-I-making-this-up-kind of way. I'm hoping you can get her to take some kind of action. I think that's why the dreams are coming to her in the first place."

"Addiction can be a tough situation," Randi said, rubbing her chin the way a scientist does when they're thinking.

"C'mon," Debbie said, leaning forward with her elbows on her thighs. "You're the expert. What do you think the dreams are telling my mother to do?"

Randi rotated her shawl at her shoulders. "I don't think one has to be a psychic detective to figure out what the dreams are telling your mom to do."

My heart stopped for a second, and then pounded in my chest, hard, as if to accentuate the moment. Slowly, I lifted my head. The room began to swirl and spin, causing a type of tunnel vision in my mind, Randi and Debbie at the center of the kaleidoscope.

Then, without warning, my hand raised in the air like it was pulled on a string by some outside force. A second later, I heard myself ask, "What's a psychic detective?"

Randi turned to me and blinked once, as if she was caught off guard by my participation. "A psychic detective is a highly skilled intuitive who works with the police to solve crimes," she said.

"Like a job?" I asked. My body temperature grew cold.

"It can be, certainly at least a job on the side," Randi explained. "I don't do that kind of work, but I know of people who do. Now, in terms of what to act on and what to let lie from our dream state, let's take a fifteen-minute break and then we'll turn to the last page and see if we can answer your questions."

A chill rippled through me, over, under, and around every cell in my body.

CHAPTER FIFTEEN

I weaved through the noisy main conference room. My body continued to shiver, like an air-conditioning unit, humming electric, vibrating cold. I glanced above the heads of vendors talking to attendees after I exited the rest room, with no intention of speaking to anyone, let alone a tarot card reader like Gwen had suggested. Just before I reached the hallway that led to Randi's classroom, a gum-chewing, Italian-accented voice rose above the chatter of the crowd. "Hey, pretty girl. May I speak with you?"

Instinctively, I turned, my body jolted out of the private space I had been in, as if someone had pulled a plug out of its socket. An olive-skinned woman with dark, cherry-red highlighted hair gestured to me with flashy, diamond-studded acrylic nails toward the empty seat in front of her table. A glossy deck of purple and orange angel cards spread halfway across the top of the small table, beside an empty mason jar for tips and another mason jar filled with water and a wedge of lemon.

"Me?" I asked, pointing to myself.

"Yes, you," she answered, her accent thick, like she grew up in Boston's original North End. With her heavy blue eyeliner and mascara, the woman appeared half gypsy-like, fitting in at the fair, and half like she might work the cosmetic counter at Macy's. "Have a seat."

I thought about telling the pushy card-reader that I had to get back to class, that break would be ending soon, but similarly to the out-of-body way my hand raised to ask the question about the psychic detective work, I found myself sitting down in the empty folding chair on the opposite side of the cream-colored, knit tablecloth-covered table, as if someone else occupied my body. I placed my tote bag between my feet and clasped my hands in my lap. The card reader's cell phone flashed 11:11.

"Don't worry," the fifty-something-year-old woman said, discarding the gum in her mouth in a tissue she kept tucked behind the lemon-water mason jar. "You'll get back to where you need to be. Spirit wants me to speak with you." She picked up the abundant deck of cards the way a poker dealer swipes them from the table to start fresh. "So, you're learning that you're highly intuitive."

I squeezed my hands tight, my legs wrapped around my tote bag, tethering me to the ground. Incense drifted through my nostrils from another table. *How did she know that? Was I being naïve? Did she assume that of everyone who showed up at a psychic fair? Or was this lady legit, able to tell me about the whole psychic detective thing?*

"I just took a class, so this is all new to me. I mean, I think I'm intuitive, I just don't know about highly," I said, scratching the bottom of my leg. I still felt as if I was speaking a foreign language, traveling in a strange land alone, which I realized is the way I had always felt, my whole life.

"You're quite guided by those on the other side, if you didn't know that already," the full-lipped woman said, shuffling the stack of cards while she stared at my face.

I bounced my leg under the table. Two women next to us purchased Mala beads from a slow-moving, hunched-over male vendor also selling pendulums and yoga mats. I thought about how Gram told me before she died that she would always watch over me. She told me to take the time to look for cardinals and dragonflies, to *always notice the signs,* the signs Gram seemed to have discovered later in life. The signs, she said, she wished she had understood and paid attention to from her own ancestors, earlier in her years.

My pulse raced, that electric feeling resurging inside me. I wanted to stand up and leave, to start researching what psychic detectives did, who they were, and if those people looked and acted like me, yet my body felt glued to the chair, as if I needed to stay seated, as if I was supposed to connect with this person for some reason I didn't yet understand.

Scratching the back of my neck, I watched as the card reader placed the deck in a pile and then tapped the top with her pointy, orange fingernail. "Select a card. I have a feeling this is gonna be good," she winked before taking a sip of her lemon water from the glass jar.

I drew from the middle of the deck and placed the stiff card beside the pile. Admiring the design of the angel figure, the gold and purple swirl of colors on the card reminded me of something I'd see in church.

"Beautiful," the woman said. She pushed the other cards aside, and moved the card I chose in the center of the table. "You drew Archangel Michael. Do you know anything about angels?"

"Not really," I said, wondering if the cards, or the lady, would provide direction as to my career path, and might be able to answer why my whole body came alive at the mention of the term psychic detective, a profession I had never heard of before today. The angel on the card grasped a large golden sword, dramatic angel wings spread wide on either side of his warrior-like body.

"Archangel Michael is the protector of children," the woman said, her elbow rested on the table, rubbing one of her long fingernails against the pad of her thumb. "He's the angel we pray to when we're afraid. This could be why you chose the card, to guide you through your fears. I sense there's been quite a bit of turmoil on your journey so far, though your aura is strong. Strong enough to handle what comes."

What did that mean? Was something bad going to happen? My forehead above my left eye began to throb.

"Often, though," the woman continued, her gaze on my downward-focused lids, "the card is selected when Archangel Michael comes to pass his sword to seekers of the truth, so they may become warriors themselves. I feel this is the case with you, pretty girl. I am being told that you need to receive the sword and to fiercely protect your gifts, in the vein of truth, in the name of justice."

Goosebumps erupted on my arms. *Gifts?* I looked up at the mysterious lady for a moment, and then back down at the shiny, biblical card, at the majestic, gold sword. *Gifts?* This didn't feel like a gift to me. Justice? *Did this have to do with Denise? Even though nothing had happened? Was the card reader secretly telling me what to do, like in code? Or was I being paranoid, looking for something that wasn't there?* The throbbing pulse spread to the corners of my forehead.

"You can call on Archangel Michael anytime for help in manifesting those gifts," the woman encouraged, continuing to stare at my face, as if she read my confusion, my overwhelmed feelings. "You have exceptional intuition, even if you don't fully understand in this moment. Your intuition is taking you somewhere in the name of service. Can you receive what I'm giving you today?" The woman placed her hand beside the card to capture my attention.

"Yeah, sure," I said. Goosebumps spread over my entire body. I didn't know what I was saying, really, or what I could or couldn't receive.

"In time, things will be clearer," the angel card reader stated in her tough chick voice before she cleared the cards from the table, causing me to release my stare. "Also in time, you'll come to recognize the resources you can call on, both in this dimension, and in the other realm, to help carry out your most purposeful work."

My feet remained glued to the floor, the rest of me racing inside myself like a puppy just let off a leash. What kind of purposeful work? It couldn't be simply working at Alante's for my father. It just couldn't. Why did my entire body temperature drop when I heard the term psychic detective?

I squinted the way I did when I had a migraine, my head heavy from every word the card reader spoke—swords, service, *using my gifts*—which, at the moment, seemed more like a burden. I had always thought of gifts as something that came naturally to someone, like the way Avo cooked or the way Gwen still looked pretty even when she had the flu.

I needed to move. I needed to get back to the workshop, finish up the day and disappear in to my mind to think, but I didn't want to come across as rude.

"Do you have a question for me before you go?" The woman asked. She straightened the cards and then set them on the corner of the table next to the water and lemon mason jar.

Was I one of those psychic detective people? I thought to myself. Images of Denise, the socially awkward cashier, the gruesome vision of what I saw happen, floated down into my mind and landed on the tip of my tongue. *Would this lady be able to guide me about my dream if I asked? Was this the right person who would finally tell me what to do?*

Immediately, a cloggy, wall-like feeling of resistance pushed against the front of my body, an invisible force preventing me from speaking, as if bearing a scrolled message in its grip that once I opened to view, its simple content read: *don't.* I inhaled deeply, this heavy weight pressing against me, that no one else could see. Grey appeared in my mind's eye then, like fog on a rainy, raw day. *Don't* and *not yet* coming from two places. *Clairvoyant. Clairsentient.* Feeling both at the same time.

I exhaled, knowing I needed to keep my question to myself. Was it because this wasn't the right person, the right time? Or was it simply because I lacked courage?

Inside my mind, I prayed. *Please, tell me what my purposeful work is, what I'm supposed to do after high school. Am I supposed to help people? How? Gram, help me to recognize the signs.*

"I tell ya what," The card reader winked, before taking a sip of her water. I looked up, half-listening, still stuck inside my mind. "I'll give you a bonus reading since a girl who looks like you must have a question about love. " She closed her eyes for a moment, smiling as if she heard a secret, and then re-opened her heavily made-up eyes.

My heart skipped a beat. Maybe she had secretly known my real question and would tell me, without my having to ask.

"You haven't met the guy of your dreams yet," the woman said, sitting back in her chair as if she had just taken a puff of a cigarette, "but he's *right there.*"

My shoulders released. "Okay," I said, politely attempting to smile, not caring at all about some guy I hadn't met yet, or anything to do with having a relationship.

"That's what my guides are telling me, anyway," the woman shrugged. She looked above my head. "Sorry, love. I gotta take this next person in line."

After I grabbed money from the wallet in the bottom of my bag and left a five-dollar bill in the empty mason jar, I pushed back my chair. "Thanks," I said, rising to leave, not wanting to showcase my disappointment in the reading.

"Oh, and pretty girl," the woman said, popping another piece of gum in her mouth.

I turned back to face the well-dressed card reader sitting cross-legged in the chair. "If any of your friends are interested, I'm here Thursday nights. The other nights," she said, as a woman wearing an overbearing fragrance sat down in the empty seat. "I work as a cashier."

My feet stopped in their tracks. I zeroed in on the card reader's face. "What did you just say?" I asked, with my neck craned.

"I said I work as a cashier," the card reader said, her lip snarled on one side like I was from another planet and had trouble understanding. "You know, ring, ring, someone who works the register in a grocery store."

CHAPTER SIXTEEN

My hands shook as I turned the pages in the packet. The words *Answering the Call*, written in bold black letters at the top of the final page. The word *cashier* reverberated in my head over and over, like spiraling through a never-ending tunnel, as Randi began the closing segment of class once everyone returned from break.

I couldn't get warm. My body trembled as if I was standing outside in February with no winter coat. I stared down at the packet gripped firmly between my hands, reading the title a second time. Underneath, the final bullet point read: *Discernment: How to Tell the Difference Between Fear and Intuition.* I didn't know the definition of discernment, but I knew fear like I knew every groove in the pen I used to write down my dreams.

The packet crumpled at the edges, where I gripped my hands tight. I became aware, in that dramatic way when you're already strapped in at a fast ride at the amusement park, past the point of being able to change your mind, that I was moving closer to something and didn't know how it would end.

"You took the workshop because some part of you wants to answer the call," Randi said, blinking several times, the behavior no longer bothering me the way it did during the first class. "You desire finding out why the Universe has chosen to wake you up, creating some mild disturbance, maybe even major disturbance in your life, to get your attention."

Elaine glanced up from the floor at the same time I did, her face like a turtle peeking out from its shell to see if it was safe.

"Congratulate yourself for opening this portal, people, and choosing to explore a multi-sensory way of living. Do you know how many individuals ignore this part of themselves, ignore their dreams, their gut reactions, and are content to live on that lower frequency?" Randi asked, her voice high-pitched, as if the thought of going forward in life that way proved absurd. "As uncomfortable as it is to open up and embrace this new realm, I hate to break it to you people, but once you start down this path, you really can't go back to living your old life."

I bounced both legs against the chair, my heart beating faster inside my chest. Everything began to speed up inside of me. Information flew at me from every direction inside my mind, *psychic detective, cashier, car accident*, the same way images streaked past Dorothy when she got swept up in the tornado.

"I have a question," Deidre declared, raising her pencil shoulder height. She drew her Adidas sneakers under the metal chair.

Blood rushed to my cheeks as I tried to control the thoughts swirling around my brain. The card reader also worked as a cashier.

That had to be a sign to say something.

But how could I be sure?

"Speak, please," Randi blinked. "I'm sure others have similar questions."

I glanced over at Deidre, trying to stay focused on the class.

"I had this dream last week, after our first class, that my boss had cancer. I work in a light fixture store. Anyway, in the dream, I saw an x-ray on the wall of a doctor's office. The doctor pointed to this dark looking spot in the area of the lungs, or the liver, I wasn't sure—I'm not good with anatomy or anything. But the main thing is, I knew it was bad. Well," Deidre said, rubbing the end of her nose with the sleeve of her sweatshirt, "I thought I knew. Like, in the dream, I knew. I woke up and I felt like something was wrong, you know, with my boss. But then, I went to work, and . . ."

I scooted forward in my chair, pressed my thumb hard under my chin.

"And you second-guessed yourself," Randi said, nodding as if she had heard this more than once.

"Yeah!" Deidre said, bug-eyed. "So, I see the guy—granted he eats donuts every day and is out of shape, but otherwise he's fine." Deidre used her fingers for quotations. "So, what do you do with that? Do I say something to him and wreck his day or do

I just keep it to myself and see what happens, which by the way, not only gives me anxiety, but also makes me feel like I'm a bad person, like if I don't say anything. Does that make sense?"

A rush of energy rose to my throat. Every part of me wanted to tell Deidre that it made perfect sense to me and made me want to share my dreams too. I tightened my stomach, trying to put the brakes on the surge of building energy inside my body. I felt I could run a marathon. More than ever I wanted to check in with Randi about my dream and see what she thought I should do about my dream involving Denise.

"It's a valid question," Randi answered Deirde. "A question most intuitives struggle with at the beginning of their journey. Here's how I've come to look at it. When the dreams won't let you go, following you around for days, sometimes weeks, nudging you constantly, causing you anxiety, that's when you act. That's when you know it's bigger than you, the dream's given to you for a reason. That's discernment."

Deidre nodded her head a few times, as if to herself. "So I'm supposed to do something. I can't get the dream out of my head." Then, turning to Randi she asked, "What do you think I should do?"

I swallowed hard.

"You have a few choices," Randi replied, staring at Deidre head-on. "You could wait on it—if you can stand the driving-you-crazy part—and see if it comes to fruition, or if you feel he might be open to such things, you could tell your employer what you dreamed."

Deidre laughed out loud, her mouth opening wide. The image of a beer-bellied, sports-watching boss, who didn't even believe in the afterlife, appeared in the sight behind my eyes.

"Or," Randi interrupted Deidre's reluctant response, raising a finger in the air. "You can ask Spirit, the Universe, God, whatever your belief system is, to take the intense feeling away from you if you don't feel you can handle it, or if you don't feel it would go well if you shared your dream. That's okay, too. Spirit knows how difficult this can be people. Some individuals are more open than others. What I have also come to know, through my own experience, if this helps you in any way, is that when we choose to act on the information, which can be quite anxiety-provoking for both giver and receiver, we often change the outcome."

My heart pounded in my ears.

"What do you mean?" Lawrence asked in a quiet voice, while he fingered the green, red-flecked crystal around his neck.

"I'll give you an example from my own life," Randi said, scooting to the edge of her chair and gathering her feet underneath the way my kindergarten teacher used to before she read during story time. "I had a dream, years ago, where I saw my brother in a car accident."

"Ay yi yi," Carol said, holding her neck stiff.

"It was bad, people," Randi said, shaking her head. "Woke me up scared out of my wits. In the dream, my brother was driving, and his girlfriend was in the passenger seat, which was the side that got hit by some truck or something, I forget that part of the dream now, but anyway, I woke up and I felt that in the dream, my brother's girlfriend had died. The car was totaled, and although I didn't see what happened to my brother, I had an awful feeling weighing on me that the outcome wasn't good. I even got a date of the accident, July 14. Except, I had the dream in February. So, that brought another level of anxiety: was it accurate, *would* it happen, on that date, or some other time? You can imagine my mind— as yours is about your boss—ran wild."

I rolled my bottom lip with my first two fingers on my right hand, listening, along with everyone else, to Randi's story.

"Did you tell him?" Deidre asked, her mouth open after she spoke.

"I did, but not the first day. I sat with it, telling myself it was just a dream. This was in the beginning, by the way, when I didn't tell a lot of people about my intuition, thinking my colleagues and friends might have thought I lost my noodle—never mind my husband, but don't worry, Carol, they do come around, the good ones anyway," Randi winked. "At that time, though, I was so afraid of what people would think. I had dreamed things like local businesses closing and things like that, stuff that didn't matter to anyone other than me to see if I was right, but when I dreamed about my brother," Randi said, clicking her teeth, "well, that was the first time I had seen something tragic. Something that I knew could really freak someone out if I said anything."

"But you chose to tell him anyway?" Carol asked, her nose still scrunched, as if something smelled bad.

"Yes," Randi replied, blinking and then fully closing her eyes for a moment. "It wouldn't let me go." I realized then that Randi must have had some kind of nervous tic, which made me feel badly that I had previously gotten so annoyed.

"How long did you wait before you told him?" Deidre asked, fiddling with the earring in her eyebrow.

I felt unease in my stomach, a mix of butterflies and nausea.

"Forty-eight hours," Randi stated. "I felt like the dream followed me around on my shoulder, taunting me. I experienced a lot of fear, and because of that, I thought it just might be plain old anxiety, something I had struggled with for years, like a lot of us do when we are intuitive. I didn't want to call my brother and burden him with something that might not be true, and might be just my own fears playing out in my subconscious, so I prayed on it, to let it go. I asked the Universe that if it was something I needed to share with my brother, I would be told what to do."

I wondered if Randi prayed to Archangel Michael.

"How did you know what to do?" Elaine asked, before coughing into her fist.

"I kept feeling anxious," Randi said. She closed the packet and then set the three-page handout on top of her Whole Foods shopping bag.

"That's it?" Carol asked, tilting her chin downward and opening her palms.

"That's it," Randi said. "I trusted Spirit to tell me—we're not talking about anything religious here, people, we're talking the spiritual, asking the Universe for guidance—to take away my fear, or tell me if it was all in my head and not something of value. I remained anxious for two days, which made it hard to focus at work. After two crappy nights of sleep, I called my brother David."

"Was he mad?" Debbie asked, the mascara on her light-green eyes faded from this morning.

"No, it was more like, 'um, ok, wow, that's messed up, but good to know.' Then we hung up the phone and went about our day."

The class sat for a few moments of silence, the heater making a humming sound at the base of the wall behind my chair. I reflected how Frankie might respond in a similar fashion. I figured it might be easier if you knew the person.

"A year and a half later," Randi said, rotating the bangle on her wrist, "my brother called in a panic, informing me he had just driven somewhere—how his girlfriend was supposed to have gone with him but decided to stay home for whatever reason— and how a guy high on drugs ran a red light, smashed and totaled his car, and how, miraculously, he didn't end up with a scratch. He then told me that *had* his girlfriend decided to go, she would have been killed, sitting on the passenger side."

Carol raised her palms in the air. "Whoa."

The rest of the class sat quietly in amazement.

I dug my nail into my upper arm to make a half-moon shape. Randi's courage had seemingly single-handedly changed the situation. Was that even possible?

"It gets better, people," Randi said, folding her manicured hands in her lap. "The date was one day after the date shown in my dream: July 15 of the following year. The Universe's time can be quite different from ours, I should point out, though I had been accurate, it would be fair to say."

"Holy shit," Deidre said, shaking her head like a dog after a bath. "You must have been glad you told him. I mean, to get validation like that, that's huge. You were right."

"Validation is a big part of this work, that's true," Randi said. "We need it, as a confidence booster, like anything else, to know we're on to something and to keep doing the work. But more importantly, I learned something after that happened. I learned to trust what I saw, and to share the information, information that had nothing to do with me, but came to me, for a reason we are not always privy to."

I exhaled quietly through my nose, trying to remember exactly what Randi had just said, wishing I wrote it on the handout.

"Do you really think your brother's girlfriend would have been in the car had you not said something? That you telling him changed the situation?" Debbie asked, blowing her bangs out of her eyes.

Randi lifted her chin, as if she was under oath. "I know so."

I rotated my ankle several times in succession, one leg crossed over the other, while I stared at the floor, my left fist pressed to my mouth. The room sounded the way it did on the morning of the first snowfall in wintertime. Did this mean I should tell the cashier, warn her like Randi warned her brother? I didn't know the cashier the way Randi knew her own family member, I fought with the rational side of my brain. I noticed the desire to ask my question was no longer there, dissipated the way the flame on a birthday candle extinguishes after you make a wish.

I'd pray on it tonight, like Randi suggested. Maybe I'd ask Archangel Michael to take away my fear, then maybe I might not have to do anything at all. The thought of talking to a mere acquaintance still made me feel uneasy, even though I hadn't stopped thinking about the vision since it erupted in my mind. Like Deidre's dream, it hadn't let me go.

"I had a dream a year ago, telling me I was sick," Lawrence uttered in Deidre's direction, before clearing his throat. "Even though I didn't feel sick at the time. Turns out though, I have liver cancer. Recently, my dreams have been showing me foods I think I'm supposed to eat, like fruit and fruit smoothies. I also dream of crystals, like the one I'm wearing around my neck. Bloodstone helps purify and detox the body. I would like to believe that my dreams are giving me alternative methods of healing, versus chemotherapy, which I'm not ruling out. I simply would like to explore other means first."

Randi smiled, as if she knew a secret. "It sounds like your dreams are guiding you in the direction your body needs to take, Lawrence."

I released my shoulders and set my feet flat on the floor. I couldn't help but feel that Randi received validation regarding Lawrence's diagnosis, as did I, recalling the dream I had about Lawrence's hand being placed across from his heart, which, I now recalled from bio class, is where the liver resides.

"I needed to know that there was something to all this dream stuff, so thank you for that," Lawrence put his hands in the Namaste position and then bowed his head to Randi and to the rest of the class.

"Dreams are often a primary vehicle for healing. It concerns me when people *don't* dream," Randi said. "That usually tells me a person is psychologically blocked, perhaps not dealing with things that need to be dealt with in their waking state."

I pressed my lips together. Dad had remarked a few times that he never dreamed.

"And on that note," Randi said as she glanced at the wall clock, "we have come to the end of the workshop. I hope you learned a few things and that you continue on the intuitive path. Namaste to you all."

The other class members bowed and then stood and stretched, conversing quietly with each other over aspects of the class. I remained seated, staring at the silver legs of the chair, mulling over the thoughts in my mind, as the rest of the class stood in conversation,.

I decided I would ask Gram later that night for one final sign, something unmistakable as to what to do about Denise, if anything at all. I peeled at a nail on my left hand. I'd also wanted a sign about the psychic detective thing. If I didn't have a dream, or if no sign showed itself to me, then I'd leave it alone.

I glanced up at the clock on the wall, knowing I needed to meet Gwen outside to get to work on time. Grabbing my tote bag under my chair, I left without saying good-bye to anyone, except for a small smile through pursed lips to Deidre on my way out of the room.

CHAPTER SEVENTEEN

The temperature outside reached nearly sixty degrees when Gwen picked me up from the psychic fair. Ten minutes later, I absentmindedly walked past Holly's antiquated barn—filled with old pinball games, children's antique furniture and dusty books, that stood detached from the old, yellow farmhouse, the back half of which served as Holly's Ice Cream Shop. I didn't know how I'd get through my shift, and the night ahead, with my now regretful plans to go on the double date with Gwen and Andrew. All I wanted to do was go home and research what psychic detectives did, and then pray to Gram one final time, asking about Denise.

I stepped up onto the uneven brick walkway that swerved to the shop's entrance, running through in my mind all that had happened during the class. I didn't even get to share the card reading with Gwen, who had stayed on the phone with Andrew the entire ride to work, arguing about some party they had gone to last night and who was flirting with whom. Maybe Gwen would cancel the plans for tonight and I could go home.

Except that I had already texted my dad, letting him know I'd be going out with Gwen after my shift. Dad seemed pretty happy, replying back that he was proud of me. After not telling my father where I had really gone the past two Saturdays, I didn't want to upset the apple cart by nixing the dating plans, even if it was going to take all the strength I had to get through the rest of the day. I knew Dad probably felt better because I showed signs of normalcy. After taking Randi's class, though, I didn't feel normal anymore—if I ever had—and now I didn't care.

Scooping ice cream along with having to make simple conversation to hordes of families and teenagers out enjoying the warm autumn day proved difficult the rest of my eight-hour shift. I kept mixing up waffle cones with cake cones and putting the wrong colored sprinkles on top of people's ice cream, barely able to hide my frustration when customers pointed out my mistakes.

At 6:30, Frankie stopped by, side-stepping his way through a rowdy group of middle-school club-soccer players and their families waiting in line.

"I don't have to wait, right?" Frankie whispered. He leaned over the counter a few feet from the blackboard displaying the daily farm flavors in pastel chalk colors of orange, green, and pink while Gwen and I feverishly scooped ice cream into half a dozen cones, sweat dripping down our backs.

"Are you an idiot?" Gwen snapped from behind the counter, her arm flexed in her black Athletica tank top as she dug into a large vat of cookie dough. "I'll get to you in a minute. God."

Frankie rolled his eyes and stepped back, closer to the blackboard, while I carefully recounted my customer's order, part of me at Holly's, part of me still at the psychic fair.

Once the soccer crew moved outside, I wiped my hands on my yellow-waisted apron and walked over to the blender station, figuring Kacey, one of the other employees at work during our shift, could take the next few customers. Preferring to be in the background, away from people I didn't know, I took the liberty of preparing Frankie's usual: a vanilla milkshake with a few Oreo's thrown in for fun, minus the extra charge for the cookies.

Frankie stepped behind the counter and rested both elbows on the wooden plank running along the left side of the shop. I twisted and closed the blender, leaving my hand on the black top while I ran the machine. "Hey," he said, "I'm meeting the team for a party later at the beach since the weather's good. Want to go?"

Just then, the back door of the shop opened where Holly and her husband Stan parked their '68 cherry red mustang in a small patch of grass. "Out of the girls' work station, Frankie," Holly ordered as she stomped inside the shop, heavy-footed in her thick walking shoes. With a bark bigger than her bite, and mottled skin from winters spent in Naples, Holly appeared meaner than she actually was.

I shut off the blender and lowered my voice. "I'm actually going out with Gwen and Andrew." Holly grabbed a dishrag off one of the freezers and began tidying splattered ice cream under the takeout windows. "Apparently Andrew's hot friend Jared will be accompanying us as well," I added, in a tone I might previously have used with my friend when things were different, and I would have been considered fun.

"Really now?" Frankie gripped the end of the front counter, making sure his feet stood outside our work area. He kept one eye on Holly, who was talking with customers in the sitting area.

I took the top off the blender and poured the creamy contents of the milkshake into a sixteen-ounce Styrofoam cup. "I'll let you know how it goes," I said. I wiped the side of the cup before handing it to Frankie, grateful for the distraction of noisy customers. Now I didn't have to keep talking about things I didn't care about.

A weird sensation settled over me like a transparent sheet, everything feeling stranger than it already did: my friendships, my job at Holly's, my life as I currently knew it. Everything suddenly felt different, as if I was watching my life from another perspective. I became aware that only half of me felt like the old me, the one contained inside my comfortable, familiar life. The other half existed in a separate, larger world standing on the periphery of my life, a world that separated me from my friends.

Frankie took four dollars out of the loose, side pocket of his gym shorts and placed it on the counter. "I may have to stop by your house late night to hear. Guy has to pass my standards, you know."

"Yours and mine both," I said, trying to keep things light. I slid the money in the register and dropped the change I knew

Frankie would leave for me in the black-and-white cow container that made a Moo sound every time you dropped change into it.

Frankie raised his drink to say good-bye to me and to Gwen, who was busy at the take-out window, and then opened the door for the next customers on his way out of the shop.

I grabbed three plastic Styrofoam cups from beside the register to make sundaes for a mom, dad, and little boy wearing truck pajamas who had stepped up next in line. I repeated the order inside my head so I wouldn't mess up, even though my mind should have been on autopilot after almost three years working at Holly's.

Gwen reached down into the freezer a few feet behind me, the small silver bells on the back of the door quieting down after Frankie's exit. "Sorry I haven't asked about your morning at the thing. Andrew made me so mad earlier. Sometimes I wish he wasn't so cute. Anyway, did you like the workshop?"

I poured hot fudge into the three cups, realizing the double date was still a go. I paused before replying, "Yeah, I just gotta process all the information. It was a lot."

Gwen scraped the bottom of the vat. "Did it help?" She asked.

"I think so," I said, my face in that concentrated pose that caused my forehead to indent. That same face prompted my father to call me "too intense" once when I worked the desk at Alante's, trying to figure something out, something now I couldn't recall. Turning to Gwen, I blurted out, "I think I might be one of those intuitive people."

"Like a real psychic?" Gwen whispered before walking over and handing a medium cone to a middle-aged woman wearing a baseball cap on the other side of the window.

"The workshop lady used the word intuitive," I replied, slowly spraying whipped cream on the three sundaes while I waited for Gwen to return to the counter. "I like that better. There was something, though, that really got my attention. A psychic detective—like a job. I want to learn more about that, like if it's an actual career."

"Oooh, that sounds cool," Gwen said. She checked her phone to see if Andrew had texted. "The whole thing is fascinating, and obviously kind of freaky, too. I mean, no offense or anything, but I wouldn't want to be dealing with that during junior year."

Acid formed in my throat. The little boy jumped up beside his parents to see if I had finished their order yet. I had wanted Gwen to ask me details, the way she used to. I wanted to see if Gwen thought the card reader being a cashier proved bigger than a coincidence. But now I didn't feel like sharing that information or that a lot of the class actually resonated with me. I didn't find it cool, or freaky like Gwen did. I found it terrifying at times, especially after taking the class. Now this whole thing felt like it was becoming a responsibility.

I topped the sundaes with cherries and set them on top of the glass counter, noticing Kacey only after she waved good-bye at the close of her shift. In the midst of my thoughts, the bells on the back of the door handle made their magical Christmas-like sound.

"Holly's must be the new donut shop," Gwen said out the side of her mouth. "We don't usually get the cops."

Immediately I looked up, past the dark wooden paneled interior walls filled with antique license plates, toward the door. Detective Len Dyer, his freckled forearms weathered like he had worked one too many details in the summer sun, and a younger police officer, standing several inches taller than Len in his dark blue uniform, entered the shop. They took their place in Gwen's line, standing behind the rowdy boys causing chaos as they grabbed their ice cream cones to go.

A chill ran through me. I knew Detective Dyer through my family. Alante's had been broken into five years ago and Len worked the case. Len had also gone to Hanley High School with Avo and my grandfather, back in the day. The other good-looking officer, as lean and fit as Len stood round, I didn't recognize.

Detective Dyer gave me a slight wave, the bulletin board on the wall behind him filled with pictures Holly took of all her employees at their junior proms over the years, next to a homemade sign in pink marker that read: Thank You For 30 Years. I took a twenty-dollar bill from the mother of the pajama-clad boy and opened the register to return the change.

"Andrew's here," Gwen squatted down beside the counter and squealed like a five year old on Easter morning. "How do I look?"

I glanced back toward the door, locking eyes for a moment with the younger police officer standing in my line of sight. The hairs on the back of my neck stood on end, until Andrew and all his muscles stepped into the scene. Strutting inside Holly's in his sleeveless black shirt, alongside a second gym rat, whom I surmised must be Jared, Andrew's beady dark eyes narrowed as he surveyed the small crowd in the shop.

"Hey, babe," Andrew said, maneuvering around the line and leaning over the front counter, making it known that Gwen was his girl. Finishing an order at the takeout window, Gwen smiled at Andrew over her slender shoulder. "Hey," he said, jerking his chin in my direction. Then he elbowed Jared, who reminded me of a tanned pumpkin in his neon-orange T-shirt and beefy arms. Jared, with his long wavy hair, smiled a cheesy smile and proceeded to scan me from the top of my side-parted light-brown hair down to my black flip-flops and neglected, unpainted toes.

"Hey," I replied, not wanting to be rude, but also not wanting to make conversation. I turned my attention to the senior couple sporting matching tan, zip-up velour workout jackets who stepped up next in my line. I tried hard not to look at Len and the second officer as my body began to tremble, the same way it had earlier during the psychic fair.

Gwen knelt down to get a box of recyclable napkins under the register, looking up at me, with one brow raised. "Thoughts on Jared?"

"He's cute," I replied, not meaning a word I said—not my kind of cute, anyway. I started on the elderly couple's order, my hands shaking. Ever since the police officers stepped foot inside Holly's, I felt overwhelmed—physical feelings I couldn't control. I didn't want to explain all this to Gwen, who already started taking Len's order. I also didn't want to tell Gwen that Andrew's friend Jared, who stood against the wall talking quietly into his cell phone like some drug dealer, made me feel like a piece of meat.

"What do you know," Gwen teased, as she walked over to the freezer. "The girl's coming out of her shell."

I handed the elderly woman her ice cream cone, the woman's crinkled eyes reminding me of Gram's—the way she used to smile. I felt bad that I wasn't like the other friendly high-school employees at Holly's, talking to customers about college tours, about high school, about the weather, or asking random questions about their customer's lives, but I just couldn't.

I scratched at my arm in awkward silence while the old man slowly stretched open his wallet to pay, wondering why I even kept this job since it didn't fit my personality. How did grown-ups feel if they had to stay in jobs they didn't like? I couldn't bear the thought of that happening to me. I planned to quit Holly's as soon as I graduated.

Making change in the register, I tried hard to avoid the officers talking a few feet away in line, finding it challenging to grasp the dollars and coins between my trembling fingers.

I had known Detective Dyer for years, what was the big deal?

Oblivious to my state of mind, Gwen handed Detective Dyer his ice cream and then hastily worked on the other officer's order, all the while whispering to Andrew up close, as Len got out his wallet.

A current of energy suddenly entered through the top of my head and spread down throughout the rest of my body. An electric charge so intense it was as if my body was a house and every light, in every room, in every corner, had been instantly switched on. A thought entered my mind then, attached to the incoming energy that if I wanted to, I could pull Detective Dyer aside right now, and tell him what I saw in my dream, in my vision, about Denise.

Bile formed in my throat. How would I say something like that? Would Detective Dyer think I was crazy? I imagined my father's embarrassment, his horror, if I said something, said anything at all to the people he interacted with on an almost weekly basis.

The words on the old *Boston Operation Street Safe Dial 911* sign on the wall blurred in my line of vision. If I was going to say something, shouldn't I tell Denise first? Wouldn't that be more appropriate? Or *should* I tell a detective, since Len might know how to help?

Hold on. What was I even thinking? My legs wobbled, like one of those unstable trees in jeopardy of snapping during a windstorm. I couldn't just walk up to a detective, a professional person, and tell him I had some dream, *especially* since he knew my father.

I held on to the counter. *Trust the information,* Randi had said. *Information that's bigger than you.* But how do you detach from the anxiety?

I felt nauseous, my head spinning like I was on a fast ride at a carnival, the rides I could never stomach like everybody else. I could never explain to people, people who teased me, that those rides didn't provide a thrill for me with their twists and dips and turns—I always felt that way, racing and unsettled inside myself. No. Talking to the detective would be too far for me to go. I had to keep this to myself for a little while longer.

My fingers slid over the Formica as my clutch began to loosen its grip. I wondered how much longer I could go, how much longer I could hold onto the dream. I tried to focus on my gratitude that the line had dwindled and I didn't have to wait on anyone else, and that Jared kept talking on his phone, unconcerned about me. But Randi had said, *when it doesn't let you go, that's how you know.* The vision wasn't letting me go. If anything, the dream seemed to be expanding inside my mind, inside my body, like a balloon being filled with air, ready to burst. I didn't know how much more I could take.

"Thanks," the good-looking police officer said, after Detective Dyer left two dollars in the cow bowl and saluted good-bye. For a split second, I felt as if the younger officer was speaking directly to me. I glanced up and the intensely building feeling released, leaving me as quickly as it had arrived, as if someone had pulled a plug on the crazy.

Frozen in place for a moment, I watched as the police officer with the straight edge nose followed Len out the door. The string of silver bells swayed back and forth, sounding their happy sound as the officers stepped back outside into the darkening parking lot.

I bit my lip hard. Had I lost an opportunity to help? Did I do the right thing by not saying something? The right thing for Denise, or the selfishly right thing for me?

CHAPTER EIGHTEEN

Later that night, around 10:00, I sat on the edge of the living room couch, texting back Gwen. I was finally about to research the subject of forensic psychics, when the front door opened.

"Home before me?" Dad asked in a surprised tone. His chair made a hissing sound as he sunk his stocky frame down into it. He kicked off his loafers, the ones he typically wore to the bars and rested his bare feet atop the leather ottoman.

I twitched my toes in my white ankle socks that doubled as slippers after I got home. "The date wasn't worth my time," I reported, continuing to text Gwen that no, I wasn't in a bad mood earlier at the local pizza place, just tired after a long day. I never got to talk to Gwen alone. She and Andrew remained glued at the hip the entire time the four of us ate—well, the three of them ate—at the restaurant.

"What does that mean?" Dad asked. His eyes narrowed as he reached for the remote lying on the ottoman, his demeanor morphing into protective mode.

A minute later, two knocks sounded against the side of the door, the voice calling through the screen, "Yo, I wanna find out about the hot date."

I squeezed my phone in my hand, just wanting time alone to start my Google searches.

"C'mon in, Frankie," Dad said, gesturing with the remote. "I wanna hear about this date too." Dad changed the channel from the local news where a dry weatherman forecasted another warm autumn day tomorrow to TruTV, landing on a recent episode of *Impractical Jokers*.

"I love this show," Frankie said as he sauntered into the room. He pulled up the edges of his red Nike shorts and plopped down on the other end of the couch, facing the television.

Distracted by the show, Frankie and Dad laughed out loud over the next few minutes at Sal's unsuccessful attempt—and his counterpart Joe's resulting hysteria—to sell a timeshare to a group of unsuspecting individuals, while I scrolled through my phone. I read one entry from some guy who called himself a psychic detective who worked with a family after contacting them through Facebook, two weeks after their teenage daughter had gone missing. The girl ended up being a runaway, returning home two months later, supposedly like the psychic guy predicted.

Dad clapped and then briskly rubbed his hands together once the show took a commercial break. "So, we gonna hear about this date?"

Reluctantly, I placed my phone down on the couch to the right of my hip, making sure the picture of the psychic detective—with balding hair and glossy round eyes that looked more like a mug shot taken at the police station than a professional photo—wasn't visible to Frankie or my father. I didn't need any more questions. "There's not much to say," I answered with a shrug. "Gwen fixed me up with Andrew's lacrosse friend, Jared. We went for pizza after work and then, not much later, I asked Gwen to bring me home."

"Sounds like a blast," Frankie said. "Kind of like the shindig out at the beach until the cops broke it up." He yawned, raising both arms overhead.

"Yeah, I'm pretty sure I won't be invited out again," I said, biting my lip, not caring in the slightest, especially thinking about how Jared had tried to put the other ear bud to his head phones in my ear so I could hear some song on his playlist. Flinching, I told him I was all set. I wasn't a germophobe or anything, but that totally skived me out.

"No sparks with jacked-up Jared then?" Frankie asked, stretching his legs out in front of him. He crossed his sneakers, with the loose, dirty-white laces, at the ankles.

"Jared's in love with himself," I said, rubbing at the center of my forehead, recalling the way he flexed at the table when he reached over to grab more napkins, as if I might be stupid enough not to notice. "And Gwen and Andrew are so in love with each other, they don't notice anyone else in the room. I don't even think Gwen noticed how rude Andrew was to the worker who came over to help clear the table. He kept piling stuff on the stack she had in her arms, like it was some joke."

"Gwen's in love, huh?" Dad chuckled. He clasped his hands behind his head.

"Gwen's in lust," I retorted, glancing down at my cellphone after it vibrated on the couch. Reactively, I turned the phone over, a text from Gwen reading:

**At least tell me you think Andrew is gorgeous.
Am I lucky or what??**

I rolled my eyes, clicked the button on the side of my cellphone case and shoved the phone in between the end cushion and the armrest.

"Yeah, that kid Jared's a piece of work," Frankie said, adjusting his Chicago Bulls baseball cap sitting high on top of his unruly head of hair.

Dad shot Frankie a look. "And you let my daughter go out with him? I thought you guys looked out for each other?"

"Yeah, what's that all about?" I asked.

"What?" Frankie scoffed, looking first at me, then my father and then back at me. "I knew you wouldn't fall for a dude who spends half his time in a tanning bed."

Dad's phone rang, that familiar Outfield song erupting in the room, capturing my father's attention. Retrieving the phone from the pocket of his shorts, my father smiled and then lightly tossed the phone beside his bare foot on the ottoman.

I flicked my ankle back and forth. Between my father and Tina, Gwen and Andrew, and Frankie and his friends, everyone seemed engrossed in their own relationships, clueless as to what was really happening in my life, beyond the meaningless double date.

A commercial sounded too loudly for my liking on the TV. I thought about the other thing the angel card reader said to me, about a relationship, and wondered if I ever would have one of my own. What if I continued to be consumed by my dreams, and my deepening intuition, a subject people in my current circle didn't really care to understand?

I chewed the side of my thumb, recalling the annoying way Jared tried to start a conversation with me at the restaurant, like he was trying to make up for the awkward ear bud interaction, while Gwen and Andrew made out on the other side of the table, something we both agreed we'd never do in public. "You should come out drinking with us one night at the beach," Jared had said, with an attempted, pathetic swag, beside the unlit gas fireplace next to our table..

I didn't share those details with Dad, who resumed watching *Impractical Jokers* with Frankie, both of them laughing their heads off when Sal discovered a picture on the screen projector of his sister getting married to Murr. Taking advantage of the distraction, I grabbed my phone out of the side of the couch to continue my research, wishing I was alone.

At 11:00, Dad pointed the rectangular remote at the thirty-inch television on the far wall that separated the living room from my bedroom and then tossed the clicker on the ottoman. As the screen darkened, Dad scratched the back of his neck, saying he had to go into the shop early tomorrow to work on inventory.

The table lamp cast a simple yellow glow in the room as Frankie replied to an incoming text, and I read the next entry about some exposed psychic detective who milked people for a lot of money.

"You still having bad dreams now that you're on medication?" Frankie asked, tucking his cell phone into the side of his zipped-up navy-blue sweatshirt.

I waited for Dad's reaction, not sure how to respond.

Dad had his eyes closed, then opened them half-mast and replied, "Devon's doing great. I'm thinking this is all behind us."

I nodded my head, playing along, making me feel almost powerful in a sneaky kind of way, since my dad had no idea about the workshop, and I hadn't once taken the medication.

"Just wanna make sure my girl Dev's all good, " Frankie said with one hand on the back of his red Bulls cap, one hand on the black brim, adjusting it just right. Then, addressing my father as if I wasn't in the same room, Frankie added, "Glad to hear it."

Dad pushed his palms against his thighs and stood, trudging over and patting Frankie on the side of his scrawny, toned arm. "Thanks, bud. It's been a good couple weeks. Dev'll get a good night's sleep and be ready for work tomorrow. Last day at the warehouse, right?"

Frankie rose and stretched both arms overhead. "Yup. I'll be here bright and early. You heard the man. Get some sleep."

I lay awake for a little while longer after I didn't find any information—legitimate information anyway—that I had hoped to about psychics who worked with the police. A few cases had popped up in my research, involving missing children. They seemed geared more toward people wanting to help out by searching locations in volunteer fashion. A few psychics predicted whereabouts of the missing kids, but they weren't accurate.

Tired, I shut my phone off and began practicing Randi's breathing exercises while going over the three levels of intuition in my head. I recalled instances when I felt something, saw something, and then, hearing my name called a few weeks ago, never realizing that all these experiences I had might have been a big deal.

With my eyes closed, as I exhaled, Denise the cashier's face appeared in my mind. I hadn't even gotten to pray to Gram, or Archangel Michael to protect me from fear, or to help me, as the angel card reader said, become a seeker of truth.

My heart beat faster while I lay still. I heard a lone car drive past outside my closed window, the sound of rushing wind leaving behind a trail of wondering. Could Gram, or maybe even Archangel Michael, already have known my prayer, without my direct asking? Did things work that way, on the other side—like they just knew?

A coiling feeling of energy raced through me, frantic, as if winding around a spiral staircase inside my body, the nightmare replaying behind my eyes every time I closed my lids. The way the cashier had laid there helpless on the floor of the oak-cupboard kitchen. No one else knew what had happened.

Except the guy.

Except me.

I opened my eyes.

I knew.

I saw what happened. I witnessed the crime like I was standing there, even though the crime hadn't actually happened. A wad of fear stuck in my throat.

But it could happen, I told myself. My eyes darted back and forth across the shadowed ceiling. Similar to how Randi dreamed about her brother.

I squeezed my toes tight, as if to step on the brakes of the coiling feeling. That surging feeling of responsibility caused my body temperature to rise and everything felt fast and forward moving, and completely beyond my control.

I pushed my covers down halfway, to my waist. So if it was true—if what I saw really happened, even though it really hadn't—I was kind of responsible for letting Denise know, for warning her if it did, even though part of me, my logical mind, realized that thought made absolutely no sense at the same time I thought it. A point above my left eye began to pulse.

I squinted, trying to release the building pressure in my brain. My thoughts returned to the car accident. I tried to convince myself there was nothing I could have done ahead of time about that situation. Yet my mind kept gently pulling me, like the tide, in the direction of thoughts like: *What would I have done if I didn't worry so much about what people thought? What I would do if I were truly brave?* Randi said an intuitive has to trust the information that comes. If I trusted myself, if I trusted the information, even though I didn't know exactly where it came from, or why it came to *me*, what would I do then?

I squeezed my eyes tighter. *Gram, please tell me specifically what to do, so I don't look like a fool.*

Lying in bed against the stiff sheets, my mind continued to race. I envisioned what Randi might do, after working with this for twenty years. Randi would probably drive right to Denise's house and have a private, matter-of-fact conversation.

I rolled over on my side. If I had my license, and if I was brave, I'd get up right now, and drive to her house. Except I didn't know where Denise lived. I could find it if I really tried, though, like if I woke Dad up and asked him to check with Tina for the information.

If I was brave, I might do something like that.

I rolled over on my other side and then returned to lying straight on my back. That would be weird, though. No, that would be considered crazy. What if Denise's family called the police on *me*? I couldn't do something like that. I'd look like a crackpot. And so would Dad.

I turned back on my left side, staring at the canister of Calm I had refused to take. The little hand on the square clock rested on the twelve, the big hand on the one. The dream had never really left me. According to Randi, that meant I needed to do something.

Something that might change the outcome.

For another half hour I tossed and turned, my mind rolling in thoughts, and possible conceivable and not-so-conceivable actions. I didn't feel any guidance from Gram or God or His Angels.

Wrestling with knowing I needed to sleep, in preparation for another long workday, I stared up at the shadows on the ceiling, my heart pounding in my ears, and made a pact with myself. Tomorrow, I'd ride my bike to the Natural Grocer after Frankie dropped me at home after work. IF Denise worked the register, I'd take it as a sign to tell her about the dream. I'd be cool about it, maybe half-laughing, like, "I know this sounds crazy but . . ." and then let her digest what I said, deciding for herself what precautions she might want to take, if any. Or she could simply decide I was a nutcase. No one would need to know other than Denise and myself. Then, at the very least, the responsibility would be off me.

I slid my right foot up to my left knee, making the shape of an upside-down four. If Denise wasn't working, I'd leave it alone and let it go.

I inhaled deeply, my shoulders tight. I had made a plan. Finally. And unless I had a dream through the night that guided me in a different direction, or a message that appeared in some other way, I vowed to stick to it.

I had to. At least it was action of some kind.

Right now though, I needed to try and sleep.

Silently, I prayed.

Archangel Michael, I've never prayed to you before and I didn't know anything about you until today, but if you really watch over kids, then please help me. Help me be less afraid. If I don't have what it takes to be brave, or to be a warrior like the kind of people you work with, then please take the dreams away.

Then, I closed my eyes for the night, not knowing how much longer I could deal with anxiety crawling the walls inside my body.

CHAPTER NINETEEN

The strumming of the harps from my phone alarm at 7:30 the following morning reminded me of what I had planned to do later that day. I blinked a few times, adjusting my eyes to the golden hue spanning across my room. I didn't recall any dreams, and actually felt refreshed, only waking once at around three-thirty. I stared at a spot on my window, my room quiet and uneventful, which I attributed to the clearing incense I had used last week.

I rubbed my eyes with the palms of my hands, anticipating the idea of getting on my bike later and riding the four miles to the Natural Grocer, after coming off a six-hour shift unloading cartons in the muggy warehouse. In the midst of my thoughts— my heart pitter-pattering as my body more fully entered into consciousness—a few, fuzzy fragments of a dream floated through my mind before evaporating into thin air, like smoke from a candle.

I tried to capture the contents, tried to remember if perhaps I had caught sight of the little girl in the nightgown again—to no avail.

Unsticking myself from the sheets, I rolled over and sat upright, pausing on the edge of my bed for a moment before getting dressed in a pair of black leggings and a raspberry long-sleeve workout shirt I hadn't worn since taking yoga at school last spring. Balancing on one leg while I put on my sock, I wondered if I ought to rethink my plan, now that daylight had arrived, the time when things became clear.

I pulled my hair back in a low ponytail with the elastic I had kept on my wrist, the one that caused grooves in my skin during the night. Then I opened my bedroom door, cell phone in hand, knowing Dad already left for work, and instead of the usual Sunday breakfast of sausages and eggs, he likely left me yesterday's blueberry muffin from Dunkin Donuts.

Still wrapped in my thoughts about the bike ride and where to tell Dad I was if he got home from work before I did, I pressed my bare feet into the flat carpet with my head down—walking past a few of my elementary school pictures hung in inexpensive gold frames on the antique-linen painted wall—everything status quo when I stepped onto the cold kitchen floor.

Except that Dad was still home, sitting at the kitchen table, staring out the backsliders without looking my way when I entered the room, black coffee mug in hand.

I approached the island; no store-bought muffins, or food of any kind, out for breakfast. My eyebrows squished together. Dad still hadn't said a word, continuing to stare outside at the half-shaded deck. Had something happened to Avo? My heart dropped. Having Type 2 diabetes and a propensity for sweets, Avo didn't take great care of herself. Did my last living grandparent pass away? My stomach tied in knots. Unable to speak, the way I often felt in school when I wanted to ask a question but couldn't because I was too anxious, I waited for Dad to say something.

Finally, after clearing his throat, in a voice quieter than normal, Dad said, "Tina called me early this morning." His bloodshot eyes remained glued to the closed glass sliders.

I shifted my weight onto my left leg. Did Dad and Tina break up? Not prone to drama, my father usually didn't concern me with those kinds of things.

Turning to face me, my father rested his forearm atop the table. A pained expression wore on his face.

"What's the matter?" I asked, pressing my toes into the base of the island to make them turn white.

"Tina's employee, that cashier Denise you dreamed about," Dad replied, his brows furrowed. He hesitated before finishing his sentence. "She was attacked by someone this morning in the resident home where she lived."

CHAPTER TWENTY

"What? How?" I asked, my mouth slightly opened after I formed the question.

I knew it. I saw it.

Dad shook his head. He didn't look at me, just stared at a spot on the floor. "That's all I know right now."

Sections of me flew away without warning, hurling like shattered glass after a car wreck.

I clenched my fists, my knuckles as white as my toes, attempting to piece myself back together.

After a minute, maybe two, I reached for my phone. Letter by letter I pressed the keys, texting Frankie not to pick me up, offering no explanation.

I squeezed the grooves in the sides of my cell-phone case, gradually reconnecting, through the ridges, to my body.

Was Denise dead?

Dad moved his heel back and forth a few times, the way someone does when they're putting out a cigarette. Then he sipped from his mug, the slurping sound the only noise in the house.

Dad's expression, the one I could never read, reminded me of the time I made a Mother's Day card in third grade, in Mrs. Gray's class—stating all the reasons I loved my mother even though she had been gone for almost three years and I really didn't know her—proudly showing the pink half-folded construction paper to my father when I got home from school. With his back turned, he stuck it on the fridge with a Goodyear Tire magnet, keeping it there a day or two before putting it away "for safekeeping." When I had asked where, he replied, "somewhere special" under his breath, though he never revealed that safe hiding place.

"Is she dead?" I asked. My throat dry and parched, the way it felt at the end of a three-mile run in a summer heat wave, when you have nothing left, and require only the most basic of things.

Dad held the World's Greatest Dad mug a few inches from his face, looking dazed and confused before answering, "No." I closed my eyes, silently exhaling, continuing to rub my thumb against the ridges on the back of my phone. "But it wasn't good."

My heartbeat pulsated in my ears.

I could have said something.

I pressed my nail into my upper arm, hard. "Will she be all right?" I asked, looking at my father.

"I don't have any more details than that," he said, squeezing one hand over both his eyes. "Sounds like she'll be okay, but

Tina said she got hurt real bad. She didn't know how, that's all she heard."

My stomach felt as if a knife plunged into its side. Did my waiting cause this to happen? My concern for myself, concerned about looking like a crazy person—did that prevent me from helping this girl? Is that what happened? Was this my fault?

My eyes darted back and forth, scanning the baseboard of the kitchen below the cupboard. If I had been strong enough, confident enough to go and tell Denise about the dream— just tell her and let her decide for herself whether she should be worried, or maybe just give her a heads up so she could have anticipated it, and then done something about it, like maybe have someone with her, or get a weapon or something—maybe things would have turned out differently.

Oh my God—what was I even saying? How had things come to this?

My leg bounced in place, my knee brushing against the island. "Did you tell Tina what I saw?"

"No," Dad said, shaking his head, as if to say *no way in hell*.

My father's solemnness, along with the pronounced dark circles under his eyes, made it hard to decipher whether he was angry or just unsure as to what to do next.

"Sit down," he said, with his eyes closed, gesturing beside him to the empty chair.

I laid my phone on top of the counter, cracked both thumbs and then crossed the tiled floor that hadn't been swept since Avo's last visit. I pulled the chair away from the table with both hands and sat down, tucking my hands under my legs. I pressed both hands deep into the straw cushion so I could feel the indentations on my palms.

"Tell me about your dream," Dad said quietly, firmly. He set his coffee down on the table, his large callused hands covering most of the white-and-red lettering on the black ceramic mug.

My entire body began to vibrate like an engine being started, the way it had during the workshop, the way it did, I now came to realize, when something important was happening.

I shifted in my chair, attempting to find some sort of centering place.

My father focused on the salt shaker and few napkins left in the holder, avoiding my face. Then he closed his eyes for a moment, the way a person does when they wish things were different.

Freeing both hands from underneath my legs, I folded them in my lap, the same way I did whenever Avo said we'd start dinner with grace. Then, looking over Dad's right shoulder, into the blue and red dainty-flowered wallpapered half-bathroom and laundry room beside my father's home office, I responded, "It was more than a dream."

A chill sprinted down my spine as I recalled the vision, experiencing a strange sensation of power while being asked to talk about my dreams. It was as if I was discovering for the first time that my body craved the question, craved the answering.

I kept my focus concentrated on a spot on the wall, speaking more to the blue and red flowers that blurred into a unified shape, than my father. "I was there," I continued, my voice in a dream-like tone. "In Denise's kitchen, or somebody's kitchen, observing what happened, as if it happened in real time. It's hard to explain to someone else. I know I was actually, physically, in my bedroom, but I was in that kitchen, too—or a part of me was. I still can't figure out how that works, or how that's possible, but I was in that house—at the same time I was asleep in my bed."

Dad's eyes narrowed, staring into my faraway eyes—searching them, analyzing me for a moment. Then, tightening his grip around the coffee mug, he said, "Denise Franklin is her name. She'd been staying in a group home off Main Street, a home for people with emotional issues. Tina worked with the home, part of community outreach or something. Said Denise was doing a nice job, you know how sweet of a kid she is." Dad looked away for a moment, toward the few napkins left in the holder, a confused expression on his face. "One of the residents called the cops early this morning when they turned on the coffee maker and found her beaten on the floor. I guess it was a bad scene." Dad set the mug on the table and swiped one hand down over his face, almost as if he might cry. "Jesus Christ."

My heart hammered wildly in my chest. Attacked. In a kitchen. *Just like I saw.* Just like they showed me. *But who showed me?* Who wanted me to see that? Who would want that for Denise, so harmless, so innocent?

Unless it was my job to help and the incident, the crime, could have been avoided.

I dug my thumbnail into my right thigh, leaving an indent in my legging.

"I don't know what to do," Dad said under his breath. He ran his hands through the top of his hair, his eyes widened, like a wild animal backed into a corner.

I pulled at my lip with the first two fingers of my left hand, and before I had the chance to think twice, I asked, "Maybe you could call someone at the station. I saw the guy who hurt her. Maybe I could help."

Dad squinted, the way a person does when the sun is too bright for their eyes to handle. "What do you think you can do that the police aren't already doing? All the suspects live in the house. They're going to figure it out eventually. You're not a detective. Besides, you can't arrest a person based on some random dream."

My throat burned. This weird feeling rose inside me like a memory surfacing of something being taken away from me—just like the time that little girl, Julie Tully, in first grade tried to take the Talking Baton out of my hands before I was done telling my roses and thorns report from summer vacation. I had held onto the baton tight, as if everything depended on my not letting it go.

"But what if I can help?" I asked. I sat straighter in my chair, pulling my stomach muscles into me. "What if something I said, or something I offered the police from what I saw, made a difference and helped the case? That's what matters most, right, helping someone?"

Dad sighed with his eyes closed. "They're gonna be busy on this case. They don't need inter—"

The blood rushed to my cheeks. "You can't expect me to sit here and do nothing. Do the police have any suspects?" *Did they catch the guy with the wild eyes?*

Dad's right shoulder twitched, several times in a row. "Denise got messed up enough that she can't, or maybe she just won't, identify her attacker. Tina told me ten people live in the residence.

The detectives are gonna interview everyone. It's gotta be one of them—bunch of crazies, people with emotional disabilities and shit. No one's come clean, though. A couple residents weren't there, gone to visit their families for the weekend."

He doesn't need to come clean. I saw him. With my own eyes. With my clairvoyant sight. I could identify him.

My mind swirled with decisions I could have made. My heart pounded so hard I felt like I had been punched in my chest. Had I secretly wanted this to happen? Had I subconsciously wanted to be right? Because, if I was right, then that would mean I was good at this, at whatever *this* was. Then I'd have more confidence and maybe I could help people.

I swallowed hard, my throat dry, hurting. *The way I hadn't helped Denise.*

My eyes scanned the maroon-painted wall behind the kitchen table. *I needed to get in touch with the police.*

"What did you mean when you just said it was more than a dream?" Dad asked. His small, red-rimmed eyes continued to probe mine that were lost in thought, pulling me back to the conversation.

"I don't know how to explain it," I said, my focus fixated on a swirl of wood patterned in the table near to Dad's closed fist. I tried to decide, at the same time, whether or not I was an awful person, whether or not I was partially responsible for Denise getting hurt. "It was more like a vision."

Dad breathed heavier and asked, "What do you mean?"

The table swirls occurred in sections, in columns I separated in my mind. "I have different kinds of dreams," I said, softly. "The one about Denise was more like watching a movie."

"You have different kinds of dreams," Dad repeated in a low tone as he raised his chin toward the ceiling, stains in scattered spots from one too many harsh New England winters. "Jesus Christ . . ." His voice trailed off.

"What's wrong?" I asked, cracking my pinky finger.

Dad shook his head, like *no no no*, then reached over and banged the table with his fist, causing the salt shaker to move an inch to the left.

I flinched in my chair, my mouth slightly opened.

My father covered his eyes with his hands, rubbing them the way I did after a nightmare.

Then, as if he couldn't sit still another minute, he stood up fast, and trudged over to the cupboard, in his black and white gym shorts and white V-neck cotton undershirt that doubled as pajamas. He mumbled as he scratched at the back of his neck. "I'm not dealing with this again. No freakin' way."

"You're not dealing with what?" I asked, my eyes narrowing.

"Your mother," Dad said, his hands to his mouth, biting at his pinky finger, "t-the hallucinations she had after she drank and took pills, in the messed up way she did things—they made her effin crazy." Dad paced back over to the table, pointing his trembling finger at me. "I'm not dealing with this shit again, you hear me?"

My brows drew closer. "But my dreams aren't because of drugs or alcohol. You know I don't do any of that, and I'm not going to. Ever. I don't understand what you mean."

Dad raised his clenched fist by his waist, shaking it several times with nothing to punch. "This is fucked up."

I turned toward the sliders, the sun's rays highlighting only half the deck. *My mom was driven crazy by stuff she saw after drinking and taking pills. Like what? What did she see?*

I pressed my heel, hard, into the floor. I couldn't just let the moment go. "Did Mom see things like I do? Like about crimes and stuff?"

Dad gripped the spindles on the back of his chair, his thick knuckles ones that had seen many a barroom fight. "I-I don't know. No one understood what your mom ranted about. That shit messed her all up." He pushed the chair under the table hard, causing it to lean back on its legs. Then he stomped behind the table toward the sliders.

Acid burned in my chest. "But did Mom see things like she was really crazy, like Mr. Coleman crazy? Or did she see things like I do?"

The tag stuck out from my father's undershirt, his wide back facing me, his right palm pressed against the wall. "I don't know, I said."

I lifted my chin, pressed up on my toes underneath the kitchen table, conscious of what I was getting myself into. "That Prius accident that happened, the one we saw at the hospital. I dreamed that happened, before it actually did, during the summer."

Dad's leg, the one that had been bouncing in place, suddenly became still. Then, without warning, he punched the wall beside the sliders with his fist. The oak shelf, holding Gram's knit dishcloths and Avo's little Merry Wanderer boy Hummel figurine that she had given to my father one Christmas, fell to the floor, breaking apart into several pieces.

I sat for a moment in my chair, too stunned to move. Then, that electric charge inside me surged stronger, as if somebody, somewhere, turned up the voltage.

"I need you to call your friends at the station," I said. I leaned over and pulled my father's cell phone toward me on top of the table. "That's what needs to be done. I need to talk with someone there, maybe Detective Dyer, at the very least just to tell him, or whoever is working the case, what I know, or what I saw in my dream. You can't deny this anymore."

Dad's face flushed, the way it looks after he's had a few beers. "I'm not denying it, okay? I just don't understand it." Dad pressed his hands into his forehead.

"I'm sorry you don't understand," I said, holding the phone against my thigh. "I don't understand why you have to go out most nights after you work all day, as if you need to be somewhere else other than here with me, but I'm not in denial, or throwing a tantrum about it. I accept you for who you are. Why can't you accept me for who I am, and the things I see?"

Dad rubbed the top of his head back and forth, talking to himself. "I can't call the cops. I can't. They know me, they come to my business."

I leaned forward in my chair. "If I had gone to that girl when I first had the dream, if I had half the guts you have about so many things, then maybe none of this would have happened."

My father pressed his closed fist to his mouth and exhaled. "You can't be serious. That girl might have told everyone you were crazy, and then y-you could have been locked up, that's what could have happened."

My posture stiffened. "Is that what you're concerned about? Your precious daughter getting locked up? Meanwhile, YOU practically had me locked up, bringing me to the hospital two weeks ago for a mental evaluation! Is that okay, because you decided to bring me? God forbid I decide my own fate. You said it yourself, I'm almost seventeen, getting ready for the real world." I gripped the phone tightly in my hand. "I actually planned on going to the Natural Grocer on my own today. This girl is laid up in a hospital after getting beaten *by a guy I saw who did it.* You can't expect me to sit here and do nothing! And I won't, Dad. I'm serious. If you don't ask your friends at the station to talk to me, I'll go there myself—just like I planned to ride my bike after work today and tell Denise while you were at the shop."

Dad clutched the sides of his hair and then stormed behind the table over to the fridge. Grabbing the handle without opening the door, he then proceeded to pace the kitchen, a fire-color red emanating around his head and neck.

I stood beside the table, holding the phone in my right hand.

After a few seconds, Dad stopped, the veins in his neck bulging. He placed one hand atop the front gas burner on the stove, the other hand pressed against his forehead, like he was checking his for a fever. Breathless, my father's voice rose in pitch. "You really want me to call the cops?"

I crossed the kitchen and handed the phone to my father. "Yes. I want you to get me in with the police."

CHAPTER TWENTY-ONE

At two o'clock, Dad and I pulled into the police station for a scheduled meeting with Detective Dyer. My father parked his truck on the right side of the lot, slightly indenting the wall of yellow-leaved spruce trees. Dad kept his head down as we stepped up onto the sidewalk in front of the rectangular-shaped building. Then as if on autopilot, he put his hand against the middle of my back the way he tended to when we went somewhere, as if to say, this is my kid, my property, *I'm in charge* kind of thing. Except, instead of the solid feeling my dad's hand usually produced when it pressed against my back, today it felt flimsy, like a puppet minus the hand.

White walls with oak-stained trim surrounded a tinted glass window at the back half of the lobby when we entered the station. A woman I could barely see stood behind the center pane of darkened glass, while a few police officers spoke to one another in the background, their voices drowned out by simultaneous conversation. The woman smiled briefly at my father and me before asking the nature of our business.

Dad cleared his throat and stepped closer to the counter, as if he were making a transaction at the bank, speaking under his breath. I looked over at a Jimmy Fund canister on the upper level counter to my left, in front of a poster advertising an upcoming workshop behind the glass that read: Don't Be The Dealer. The fifty-something-year-old lady, with her pointy finger, instructed Dad and me to head down the hall about ten feet to a door that led to a series of offices and a private conference room.

Framed pictures of the town of Hanley hung on the right-side wall past the main entrance. A bulletin board hung cards from local kids thanking police for their service and a large sign reading Happy National Superhero Day signed by the kids of Cedar Elementary. My father's discomfort was palpable as we approached the door, especially after we ran into an officer my dad knew. A lieutenant named Brian briefly shook my father's hand and gave him a pat on the back before heading to the other side of the building, my dad offering no explanation for why we were there. I, on the other hand, felt oddly normal. The station felt weirdly familiar, in a way that made no sense to me, but yet total sense at the same time. A thought entered my mind that I felt more at ease here—where I knew no one, and had never been in my life—than I did at Hanley High.

Detective Dyer spotted my father. "Hey PJ, Devon," he said, rising from a chair in a small corner conference room. He gestured for us to enter the simple room with cream-colored walls, windows with navy blue valences, the venetian blinds to all four windows closed shut. "This is Bobby Dempsey, a recent graduate of the academy and my new protégé on the force."

Beads of sweat formed on the small of my back. "Hi," I half-waved. I took the seat next to my father on the opposite side of the table from Detective Len and his colleague, whom I had seen just last night at Holly's. An aerial view of Hanley during autumn hung on the wall to the right of the windows behind them. Sitting on the edge of my seat, I clasped my hands between my knees.

"Nice to meet you," Bobby said in a quiet, confident tone. He reached diagonally across the table, military-like, shaking my father's hand first and then mine, his eyes resembling the same calming, blue-green color of the ocean in tropical locations on the internet.

I awkwardly shook the handsome officer's hand, sensing my father's eyes bear down on Len's counterpart. Silently, I reflected on the fact that he had what Dad called a "respectable handshake."

"Thank you both for coming in," Len said, in the same way a person would offer you another piece of dessert at their dinner table when you were a guest. Len sat back down and pulled his chair closer to the white table that reminded me of a smaller version of the ones in the school cafeteria.

A light blue color swirled behind my eyes, informing me that this was the tone Len used when he needed to get people to open up during conversation.

My heart drummed inside my chest as Dad cleared his throat and then set his naturally-tanned, muscular arms on the table. "Thanks for taking the time. Must be a busy day for the both of you guys, huh?" He looked over at Bobby. "Len tells me you're gonna make a good detective."

"Thank you," Bobby responded, in a serious yet appreciative tone. He tapped the pencil of his eraser on the table across from me and then, noticing the sharp point sticking in the air, brought it down level between his fingers like he was playing pool.

Dad turned to me, seated on his right. "I mentioned to Len you have something on your mind that's weighing you down." He shifted in his chair, making a sliding sound against the carpet.

I blinked, parted my lips, but no words came out of my mouth.

Detective Dyer laid his short forearms, sticking out from his pale yellow short sleeve, on the table, his worn shirt appearing in need of a good wash. "Tell me about your dream, honey," Len said in a clear, commanding voice that also struck a chord of caring and concern. I imagined Len Dyer to be the best grandfather in the world.

Do not blow this, I told myself. *This is your chance.*

The light blue color stretched like taffy in my mind . . . *there's so much to tell.*

All eyes in the room were on me. Yet, as nervous as I felt, it was a good kind of nervous. To hear a real detective ask me about my dreams, really interested in what I had to say, as if I might be able to help, caused a lightness in my body I had never experienced.

I gripped my toes in my sneakers. I had to pull myself together. Pressing my hands under my legs into the navy blue zig-zag fabric of the chair, I stared at a white cord on the bottom of the venetian blind. Then, I began to tell Len about the vision.

Slowly, methodically, I described the dingy, dimly lit kitchen where Denise had been attacked: The ashen-white dishrag heaped on top of a sloppily grout-filled, cream-tiled counter; the white and silver stove displaying one rusted pine-green teakettle located on the right side of the room; light oak cabinetry with copper-hammered hinges lined the left upper and lower walls; the closed oak back door with the tinny black doorknob that I sensed led to a narrow stairway, with twelve stairs—something about the number twelve anyway—between the first and second floors of the house.

I recounted how a wild-eyed man, with sandy, sweaty hair, wearing a ring with a silver skull design, entered the kitchen from that stairwell. How he felt, to me, to be Denise's boyfriend. The attack happened fast, I explained. Denise was confused, stunned actually. Then, the guy, hammer in right hand, began to attack.

I closed my eyes, wincing at the image.

Then my legs started to shake underneath the table. I realized that was the first time I had spoken in complete detail about the vision.

I opened my eyes and sat in silence for a few seconds, staring at a different spot on the wall.

Droplets of sweat gathered on my father's forehead, the same way as when he had to work inside the service station during the summer. Bouncing one leg under the table, Dad exhaled into his fist, waiting for Len to respond.

I blinked and turned to face Len, avoiding Bobby's face, since he seemed fairly close to my age, and had to be judging me across the table in private.

Len never removed his eyes from me as I recounted the scene. He scratched the back of his whitish grey hair, the way scientists do when they're trying to solve an equation, and then glanced over at Bobby for a brief moment before turning back to me. "I need to ask you, young lady, have you ever been inside the Chase group home here in Hanley?"

Dad shook his head, his lips pursed, in mock sarcasm. "Devon's never been in there."

"Devon?" Len asked, lowering his head.

I shook my head. "No."

Len's eyes squinted, concentrated in thought, like detectives who have that same look on television. "Well, young lady, you described their kitchen."

I stared at Len's ruddy cheeks, then turned to my father, my legs flimsy, like Jell-O.

"So, you're confirming for me that you've never been inside the Chase group home?" Len asked, his chubby hands clasped on the table.

I nodded a couple of times. "Yes, I'm confirming that."

"All right," Len continued, "I'd like to show you some snapshots, license pictures and such, to see if anyone matches the person in your vision. That okay?" Len looked toward Dad first, giving him the respect he obviously felt my father deserved.

"Sure," I answered, not before looking at my father, who sat with his mouth slightly opened. Nodding once, his face grimaced, as if he felt he had to respond and had no other option,

Dad appeared more uncomfortable than the time Ho number thirty-something crashed one of our family cookouts, cursing my father for standing her up one night at a bar.

I released the position of the tips of my shoes pointing into the rug and set my feet flat on the floor. *Vision.* Len used the word vision like it was part of normal conversation. Then I pressed my left foot against my right heel and flicked my ankle back and forth. Or was Len baiting me, testing my mental health to see whether or not I was having hallucinations and wasn't in my right mind?

Bobby retrieved a manila folder from a briefcase that hung on the back of his chair.

My mind wandered. I wondered if the square-shaped watch on his left wrist was a gift from his parents, or maybe his girlfriend, when he graduated the police academy.

Sssss. Bobby slid the folder in front of Len. I noticed his fingernails, like mine, were chewed low.

Bobby's anxious in his own way, in a way perhaps most people never see, I thought to myself, the information coming to me fast, from that other place.

I scraped my foot against the floor, stopping the thoughts.

Len opened the file folder, perusing its contents.

Dad exhaled audibly and then with narrowed eyes asked, "Police don't talk with people who have dreams on a normal basis, right? I would think that's, you know, weird. Devon's a normal teenager—gets good grades, works part-time, you know, a regular kid."

Len flipped though some paperwork in the folder and then addressed my father, whose hands were squeezed together so tight

I could see the contrast of red and white from blood constriction. "I know Devon's a good kid, PJ. I wouldn't be here if I thought she was one of the cat weirdos who called the station every month saying they know where half our cold cases are located because some voice told them." Bobby looked down, chuckled. "So, do I deal with this on a daily basis? No. Sometimes though, there's good solid information that comes from those who have the gift. I'm not saying this is one of those times—no disrespect to you young lady, but being a detective for more than thirty years, I've learned to keep an open mind."

The gift.

Len had used the word *gift*.

The same word the angel card reader had used when she told me to *fiercely protect your gifts, in the vein of truth, in the name of justice.* Butterflies released in my stomach, causing a queasy, euphoric feeling.

Dad ran a hand through his hair and stared at the empty space of table in front of him.

Len selected a few sheets of paper from the folder while Bobby carefully moved out of the way a box of pencils that had been left on the table. "I'm going to lay eleven pictures in front of you," Len said, spreading the photocopies across the table, one next to the other. Barely any space was exposed in between the sheets of paper. "Some of the pictures are of random people, and some are actual residents at the group home where Denise lived, which I can tell you, is the current focus of our investigation." Len reached across the table and placed the tenth and eleventh prints directly in front of me, his face red from the exertion.

A gummy, pink-red color formed in my mind.

Len might have high cholesterol. He needs to keep that in check.

I shrugged my shoulders to my ears, in an exaggerated stretch, to cease the thoughts, acting like I was simply cracking my upper back. Information, I realized, was coming at me from all directions, flowing down like rain. I felt like this was my stage, my place, the way athletes must feel on the field, and how smart kids felt in the classroom.

"Take your time," Len instructed.

My eyes scanned the faces of the eleven photographs.

Immediately, I pushed aside the six female photos, stacking one picture of a red haired woman with dry, flat-ironed hair—*works at a coffee shop, smokes cigarettes to stop anxiety*, fast-paced, detailed thoughts about the woman running rampant in my brain—on top of a picture of a frail, petite lady who looked to be in her mid-fifties. *This one lived in an artist's community once, until schizophrenia struck.*

A buzzing feeling occurred around my scalp, as if an antenna extended from the top of my head. The thoughts were coming to me in ways they never had before—fast, difficult to slow down, hard to control, like hyperactive kids competing for attention. It was as if the thoughts had been waiting for me to notice them— these types of thoughts, for this type of situation. I didn't say anything out loud to Len, the information too hard to organize. Besides, I figured this other information had no bearing. I tried to focus only on the finding the person I saw in my vision.

My eyes darted from photograph to photograph. I felt like each person was speaking to me, wanting to tell me their story. Just then, a bigger feeling thought, like a lightning bolt striking down from that somewhere else place, burst into my brain, causing all the other, detailed thoughts to scatter. The bigger thought informing me that if I wanted to know more, if I was interested in the details of a person's life, with a purpose of helping someone, I *could* get the information. It would be available to me—in order to help people.

A gift.

I squished my toes together and gathered the five remaining photos with a reverence I never had at Holly's serving ice cream, or the warehouse loading shoes, or organizing paperwork at the front desk at Alante's.

With weird confidence, I set the snapshots in front of me, in a row, lined side by side. I dragged the photo on my far left, of a guy, closer to me, placing it between my hands. Dark hair. Beady eyes. This person had the propensity of doing some bad things. I could tell.

I felt that truth.

But he wasn't the person who harmed Denise.

I pushed the photo toward the female pile, the way you'd discard a poker card, betting on the cards I still held in my hand.

The next picture I selected showcased a long-haired male, a screwy expression on his face. *Musician.* Immediately the color black clogged my mind. *A music note? A G Clef?* My head began to buzz. *Something mentally off, something chemical going on.* Wait. *Too much medication?* My mind swarmed with activity, like a beehive. A pulsing feeling behind the black color called to mind little minions attempting to beat down the wall of black, clamoring for my attention, like it was important.

Squinting as if to see better behind my eyes, I sensed this guy lived at the group home, but the guy I saw in the vision had different color hair, a different face. No, this wasn't the person.

My head dully ached as I became aware of how much brain effort it took to do this type of task, like studying for finals in a crammed amount of time, except that I was interested in the subject.

I moved the photo into the messy pile of nine.

Photo number three featured an older guy, around Len's age, sporting a scruffy beard. I stared down at the picture. The words *convenience store robbery* plopped into my head, the way one thick droplet of rain does before it starts to downpour. Was that clairvoyant or clairsentient? I could kind of see it, but felt it too. I couldn't be sure. That feeling again that I could receive a boatload of information on this guy, if I concentrated hard enough, if I wanted to.

If I wanted to.

The area above my left eye beat hard, a bass drum, playing the same note over and over. No, I didn't want all this extra information. I couldn't distract myself with the other snapshots. I still needed to find my guy. I felt like I was feeling the positive effects of stress, at a "job" I liked, something, for the very first time, that I felt good at and that seemed natural.

I rubbed my feet back and forth on the floor. *What was I learning in high school anyway? Was it even relevant to me and my life?* Thoughts weighed down on my mind, piling up one on top of the other, the way Sunday newspapers do in the plastic bin in the front hall after a few months.

My brain grew heavier, my mind getting tired, distracted. I pushed the picture of the bristly bearded guy into the rising pile.

Two photos remained. With my first finger, I slid the second to last snapshot to the rim of the table. A smiling young man, around the age of 25, wearing round glasses, stood next to a pine tree, similar to the way senior pictures are taken in high school.

My body temperature dropped.

I began to shiver, realizing now that my body exhibited this behavior whenever I felt myself become truly alive.

Standing next to the tree, I noticed the wrinkles in the man's eyes, the same wrinkles that creased when he held the hammer above Denise in his unstable hand. This had to be Denise's boyfriend, the exact same guy I saw in my dream.

I stared at the photo, my lips parted. I had never seen this person in real life, only in a dream. Yet there he stood, a real person, in real life.

How did that happen? How could you pick up on things like that? Could everyone do this? Was that the gift? To see something before it occurred? Or was it in the helping?

"What's your sense?" Len asked, elbows rested on the table, his shoulders hunched.

Dad shifted uncomfortably in his chair.

I looked over at Len. "That's him."

Bobby glanced to his left, at Len, who kept his eyes on me, his hands folded together on top of a stack of paper, a blue, ballpoint pen an inch away from his wrist. "The one in your dream?"

I nodded a few times. Then I looked down one more time at the picture, at the guy who appeared happy, not like some perpetrator who'd hurt anybody on purpose, and definitely not someone who'd possess a skull ring. What had happened to cause this person to behave the way he did in my vision?

What was his story?

My mind raced. Did I want to go deeper? Could I do that, just by asking? Could I make the information happen on purpose? Or did it just happen naturally?

My thoughts bounced back to Denise, lying in a hospital bed. I blinked, erasing the extraneous thoughts. "Yeah," I answered, crossing my ankles under my chair, pulling myself closer to me as if I was a turtle retreating into its shell. "That's the guy."

Len pressed his finger on the remaining picture on the table. "Do you want to check the last photo?"

I shook my head. "No."

Dad wiped the end of his nose, making a sniffing sound, even though he didn't have a cold.

"Okay," Len said. He swiped all eleven photos in a more cohesive pile, organized them neatly and placed them back in the original manila folder, which he then handed to Bobby. "I think we're done here."

I sighed, my head bowling-ball heavy, like how it felt when I used my cell phone for too long.

Dad looked like he'd been slammed by a Mack truck. He sat silently in the chair, the veiny blue lines under his eyes more pronounced now that he had been up for almost twenty-four hours.

Bobby slipped the folder back into his briefcase as Len pushed back his chair and stood, retrieving a business card from the pocket of his yellow shirt. "Thank you, young lady. If you think of anything else, don't hesitate to give us a call." Len placed the crisp card on the table and gestured for Bobby, in the middle of rising from his chair, to do the same.

"So, can you tell us anything more, Len?" Dad asked, rising from his chair. His brow furrowed, lines in his face I never noticed pronounced under the artificial light.

"I can't say much," Len said. He rested his hands on the rounded back of his chair. "We already have a couple suspects in mind who reside at the group home, but I'll certainly take Devon's information and add it to the investigation. Should be wrapped up within the next couple days. It's not like we're out looking for a serial killer." Len slid his chair under the table.

I leaned forward with hunched shoulders, unable to let Len go without knowing. "What was she like?" I blurted out. I heard myself speak with authority, as if I had a right to know—the same way I did when I told Jared I was "all set" when he tried to kiss me after the double date outside Panera.

Len's face softened. "Well, we know Denise had a form of autism, though fairly high-functioning. Other than working part-time at the store, she mingled only with her peers at the residential home. Her mother said she had recently taken up with another resident there, who has since gone to stay with his mother and whom we have yet to interview." Len gazed into my eyes, giving me what he could.

I waited a moment, wanting, longing, to ask more. What did Denise like for breakfast? What kind of shows did she watch on television? Even though she had autism, did she like to go clothes shopping with her mother? But I didn't ask those things. I sat quietly with my hands in my lap, my questions and thoughts tangled up in my mind like a ball of yarn, forming a knot of unknowing that would have to wait, or perhaps never be untangled at all.

Dad cleared his throat. "Thanks, Len. Appreciate you taking the time. Maybe Devon'll feel better now that this is off her mind. I hate seeing her upset, you know?"

I stood, pushed my chair under the table.

"You're protective," Len acknowledged, lowering his head. "I understand, even now with my two girls having families of their own." He glanced down at his watch. "Four o'clock. Hope you're able to catch the Patriots game, PJ. If I have any questions, Bobby or I will be in touch."

Bobby straightened the box of pencils at the end of the table, my mind pulled back for a brief moment into that trance place. *Polite, but not a pushover. Strong boundaries. A sense of righteousness. My kind of person.*

I shuddered for a second, my forehead beginning to throb.

"I'll see you both out," Len said, starting for the door.

"Len," I said, causing him to turn, his neck visibly stiff. "Thanks for listening to what I had to say."

"You're welcome, young lady," Len replied before grabbing the door handle.

Bobby shook Dad's hand and then reached across the table toward me. "Nice to meet you," he said with a smile, like he meant it, his hand warmer this time.

"Nice to meet you too," I said, kind of liking the way his hand felt, hoping Bobby didn't find me too weird.

A few minutes later, Dad and I sat waiting in the truck for a few cars to pass before pulling out onto Route 139 toward

235

home. When it was clear, my father solidly pressed the gas pedal and turned left. "How did you friggin' know all that?" he asked, speaking above the agitated sound of the accelerated engine.

I stared out the window, across the street toward a beat-up little mart with Keno signs taped to the window. "I don't know," I muttered, mostly to myself. "I haven't figured that out yet."

CHAPTER TWENTY-TWO

At 5:00, after Dad had gone to meet Uncle Rob at the local pub to watch the game and "get his mind off things," the house phone rang. Avo's programmed number rang out in the living room, reverberating against the sides of my overactive brain. I felt like an adult who had just returned home from a long day of work.

I reached down and picked up the receiver I had tucked in between the cushions of the couch, stashed there in case Dad called with an update from Tina, not that he said he would. In typical Avo fashion, my grandmother never mentioned the situation, acting like nothing happened. She told me she simply called to tell me she loved me and that she had decided, on a whim this morning, to make my favorite meal of sausage soup this morning, and that Dad would bring it over after the Patriots game.

I got up off the couch and paced the small room, completing three circles before I felt dizzy. I knew Dad had to have said something to Avo. I pictured my grandmother's hand on her heart while she spoke to me over the phone, fidgeting with her fake pearl necklace, fretting over my dreams. Now that I knew my mother saw things too, even if it was after taking drugs, I figured that also meant Avo had known this about my mother.

I cracked the knuckles on my right hand. Two cars passed one after the other outside on the street. Why did my family always keep things about my mother from me? This jumpy, impulsive part of me wanted to say something right then and there, to ask Avo why, and put her on the spot while I waited, as patiently as I could, for my dad to call with information about Denise's case. Another part of me, though—maybe the same scared part that didn't want to go to the Natural Grocer when I should have—didn't want to say anything that might cause my grandmother to have a heart attack or something. I knew Avo secretly worried about my anxiety, and my migraines, blaming them on my periods each month, even though they didn't necessarily occur around my menstrual cycle.

After we hung up, and I told Avo that sausage soup would be great, I wondered how long it would take before word got out that someone who worked in our fairly small town got attacked in a way that required hospitalization.

At 5:30, I received a text from Frankie:

WTF

I flicked my ankle back and forth as I sat on the couch. I didn't feel up to talking to my friends verbally on the phone at the moment. Feelings of guilt for not saying anything, along with the secret pleasure of being right, made me feel more bad than vindicated.

Besides, Frankie knew how I could be, shutting myself off for days at a time. A black cloud sometimes settled over me, causing me to feel like I was stuck in a space between two worlds, a state I knew that Dad had always attributed to my not having my mother.

I bit at a hangnail on my thumb, recalling the first time I entered that stuck place. Kindergarten. Ally Arsenault's mother had come in for the morning mystery reader activity. Ally did this squeezing thing when she saw her mother inside the colorful, construction-paper-project-filled classroom. Holding onto one of the desks, my classmate clenched her jaw so hard all you could see was her bottom row of teeth, standing in pure bliss at the excitement of seeing her mother.

Instantly, in a whoosh-like sensation, as if someone whisked me up into a tree and had me look down on the event from a higher perspective, I experienced Ally's happiness, her soaring surge of joy, as if it were my own.

But then, that's when it happened—just as quickly as I felt her happiness, a wave of blackness crashed over me, casting me into reality. I stood alone in that spacious classroom on the second floor of the Center School building, knowing I would never, ever get to feel the way Ally did when her mother surprised her by coming in to read *The Best Nest*.

In the slamming of the opposing feeling, I found myself thrust into that space. The space that shielded me from the truth, I suppose, that I was the kid whose mother took her own life, for reasons I might never understand.

Whenever I got trapped inside the space, which was the best way I could describe the feeling, it was as if I was being held hostage. I always just said I felt sick. Dad let me stay home from school, writing notes with no problem, not worrying about what school would think or say, going off to work, allowing me to be, just sick at home. Thinking about that now, I realized it must have been easier for Dad to do things that way, to not take the time to ask me if anything else might have been going on, kind of the way Dad left today and went to watch the game with Uncle Rob, like he needed a break from everything that had happened. His need to escape took precedence over my needing an anchor.

Frankie and I texted back and forth, which resulted in my agreeing to meet in the tree house around 6:30, after Frankie got back from practice. Clutching my phone in my hand, I figured, at the very least, having some kind of distraction versus just waiting to find out if any progress had been made on the case, and if the status of Denise's condition had improved, might be a good plan.

Frankie's mother had told him about Denise, having been on duty at the emergency room when the "victim who worked in Hanley" was admitted. Frankie said he'd let Gwen know that he called the Mandatory Tree House Meeting, just in case Gwen had planned yet another night out with Andrew.

The three of us always held our Mandatory Meetings in the tree house when something was serious, like in ninth grade when Gwen's older sister was hospitalized for an eating disorder. Gwen's parents had been so preoccupied with Livvy, Gwen felt invisible a lot of the time. Knowing her parents had enough to deal with, Gwen never told them how she felt. Although we never painted our planned "What Happens in the Tree House Stays in the Tree House" motto sign, that became the unspoken rule over the years. Nestled high up above the yard, burrowed in among the oaks—the tree house was where the three of us shared secrets.

Crossing one leg over the other, I asked Frankie not to tell Janice about my dream. I didn't want anyone else in my life to know, maybe because I didn't want someone to ask me why I didn't say anything, as if someone might think the exact same way I did.

At 7:20 that night, I sat half-on, half-off the braided rug in the tree house, feeling restless after talking for almost an hour with Gwen and Frankie. At first we talked about my dream and Denise and the disbelief my friends had that something like this could have happened in real life. When I wondered aloud if I'd even find anything out at all, Frankie referred to some cop show on TV, saying they probably didn't share information with outsiders for legal reasons. Anxious that might be true, I texted my dad to see if there were any updates. He didn't answer.

The rest of the time Frankie talked about the party he went to the night before and the amount of beer the football team went through, and Gwen shared how Andrew wanted her to stay over at his house next weekend if she could figure out how to get away with it. The light on Old Man Coleman's back porch switched on, interrupting our conversation, casting a yellow glow across my backyard.

I stared at a section of illuminated grass, thinking more about the guy I saw in the vision, the one who I saw attack Denise. What happened to people that they just lost it like that, and went batshit crazy like Dad said happened to Old Man Coleman? What happened in someone's brain or life situation that they just allowed the entire spool of themselves to unravel, without leaving anything left to grab onto? I wanted to talk about this stuff with my friends, but I knew as much as they cared about me, they were more interested in their own situations.

A few lone birds flew back and forth across the yard, their occasional chirping sound creating contrast to the slamming of Mr. Coleman's back door. A moment later, I heard the familiar sound of grumbling and mumbling, Mr. Coleman performing his nightly ritual of leaving food out for the feral cats.

"The black magic ceremony's starting," Frankie said, adjusting his Pittsburgh Steelers wide-brimmed cap. "We better get going before Old Man C casts a spell on us for being out here messing up his mojo."

"Stop," Gwen said. "Mr. Coleman's not coherent enough to know anything about black magic, which isn't even real, by the way."

"Dude, have you seen that red lady on *Game of Thrones*?" Frankie asked, leaning to the side.

The door slammed a second time, prompting Mr. Coleman's porch light to go dark.

"I better go," I said. I stuffed my phone in my back pocket, unable to sit another minute and talk about shallow things. "My dad's supposed to be home soon. Hoping Tina found out more information." I crawled toward the ladder.

"Your dad is Boss Man. If anyone can find out, it's him. Hey, maybe the cops already got the guy," Frankie said, scrolling through his phone. "They haven't updated it on Twitter, though. Shit! I don't want to see the score of the game."

"You better let us know as soon as you hear anything," Gwen said, using her hands to press up and out of her seated position. "I have to study for chemistry, anyway. It's going to be a late night."

"That would suck being in honors," Frankie said, moving out of Gwen's way. I gripped the sides of the ladder before making my way down.

"If you want to get into a good college, you have to take challenging classes," Gwen said, rolling her eyes as she crawled on all fours toward the opening of the tree house.

"If you're you, then yes," Frankie said, squatting up on his heels. "As for me, I gotta go watch the Pats game that Janice so kindly taped for me so I could come chat with you little dudes. Because you know, my mother rocks. Most days."

"Your mother does rock," Gwen said, turning her head to Frankie. Then, she looked at me as I gripped the sides of the ladder, my feet on the fourth rung from the bottom. "Honestly, Dev, this whole thing really is amazing."

I smiled through pursed lips and continued down the ladder.

"You can go first," I heard Frankie say to Gwen.

"Nice manners, for a change," Gwen said. She scooted around and stepped her thinly padded flip-flops down on each rung. Frankie followed last, jumping off the ladder halfway, down onto a mossy, dark section of grass.

Gwen hugged me and then tapped the lid of Frankie's cap. "Let's go," she said. She pressed the flashlight app on her phone to highlight their way down the small wooded path leading to their subdivision. Frankie gave me a brief bear hug and darted off to follow Gwen.

Cold blades of grass brushed against my ankles as my sneakers crunched across the lawn toward the shadowy back deck. Under the waning moon, my house stood dark and still. I entered through the sliders and switched on the kitchen lights. I sat at the table, hoping Dad would be home soon, with some type of news, from either Tina or Len. Planning to wait up, I hoped he wouldn't stay out late. I started to realize that's what my father did when he found it too hard to deal with what was happening.

CHAPTER TWENTY-THREE

Two days later, on Tuesday afternoon, I scrubbed the counter repeatedly in the same spot at Holly's during our after-school shift. Gwen shut the takeout window after she waited on a customer, asking me under her breath if I had heard anything on the case.

I hadn't, other than a report on the local news that "an employee of Hanley's Natural Grocer and a resident of the Chase Group Home was severely beaten around 4 a.m. last Saturday night, the suspect of which is still under investigation."

"Who knows if I'll even hear back from Detective Dyer," I answered, applying extra elbow grease to remove a caked-on drop of fudge from the countertop. The local country station played softly in the background. "Maybe what Frankie said is true. It's not like the police have to tell us anything." I heard myself repeat what Dad had said to me when he came home buzzed the other night after the game, stashing the cold sausage soup in the fridge.

Gwen peered out the side window, behind the blender station, to see if Holly and Stan had left for their weekly errand run yet, since we had to make sure they were gone before we changed the radio station. Holly's husband lived and breathed country music. "I'm sure they'll tell you," Gwen said, retrieving a container of vanilla ice cream from the freezer so she could fill her customer's order. "Who knows, maybe they'll want you to become a real detective, and you'll go to school for criminal justice."

I stayed quiet as I stacked Styrofoam cups into two columns on the counter, business slow nearing the end of the season. I didn't want to talk about the idea of the whole psychic detective job, since I still didn't know much about what that entailed, and if it was even an option.

"By the way," Gwen said, setting the container of vanilla next to the empty one. "I had fun last night. I realize the topic wasn't light-hearted or anything, but it felt good to hang out, just the three of us. It's kind of been a while."

"I know, right?" I said, adding a few plastic spoons to the half-filled cup beside the register.

"Speak of the devil," Gwen said. She rotated the gallon of ice cream in place and wiped her hands on her pink apron as the entrance bells jingled.

Frankie strutted to the counter, the strap of silver bells swaying erratically under the doorknob. "Any word?" Frankie asked, resting his arms on the glass counter. Outside, Stan's mustang drove slowly over the dirt parking lot, paused at the exit to Route 58, and then turned left toward Shaw's Supermarket. "Hey, Stan's gone. Hip hop on."

Gwen finished making change for her customer and then switched the twangy music to the local hip-hop station. "Nothing yet," I answered Frankie. I scooped a plastic spoonful of pistachio ice cream into my mouth to distract myself from my thoughts.

"It's going to end up being the guy you said," Gwen commented before taking the next order at the window. "I have faith in you."

Frankie stepped around the counter after Gwen started talking to the group of freshman with their crisp, LL Bean backpacks arriving from school. "I stopped by the Grocer earlier to get some protein powder and you know, just to see what was up. If it wasn't a weird, hemp vibe before, you should feel it now, dude. No one said anything, but it just felt kind of freaky, knowing that lady got beat up, or whatever happened."

My phone buzzed beside the register. I picked it up and saw a text from Dad stating he'd pick me up at 5:30 after my shift and we'd go for a bite to eat. My stomach felt queasy. I knew my father had heard something about the case.

Later that evening, after we placed our order at the Four's Bar and Grill, Dad started the conversation by telling me how Danny had called in sick at work for the past two days, how he had a lot to do at the shop and that he was sorry about staying out the other night late and that "old habits die hard." My father then proceeded to tell me, after taking a long swig from his sixteen-ounce dark-beveled glass of Pepsi with crushed ice, that Tina told him the cops had identified Denise's attacker.

Except it wasn't the guy I saw.

Laughter erupted at the bar a few feet away, two roly-poly businessmen sharing some story while the television screen played above their heads next to an elongated row of hard liquor. I set the glass of ginger ale I had in my hand back down on the shellacked wooden table, feeling the room spin.

Another man residing in the halfway house, Dad went on to explain—an aspiring musician who had a psychotic break after not being compliant with his medication—thought Denise, who was responsible for meal prep duty that week, had poisoned his food. That's why he beat her with his fists and tried to strangle her to death. Until he heard the beeps of the daily trash trucks pulling up around the back of the house at 5:30 that morning and started freaking out at what he had done. He took off after that and hid in his brother's attic in Hinsdale, a few towns away. Guy acted out of paranoia. Not a romance gone bad or anything like that. Tina told my dad that thankfully Denise would be okay, but she was obviously shaken up. The Hanley police would be releasing the information to the local media station this evening.

Dad lifted his chin when he was done talking, almost as if he was secretly satisfied that I didn't get things right, as if that made him feel better for some reason. Then, he picked up the double cheeseburger the waitress had delivered to the table while we were talking, and took a bite.

My stomach hurt as I stared past my father's left shoulder, past the two guys sharing laughs at the bar. *An aspiring musician. Not her boyfriend?* I had seen a musician type in the queue of photos. I remembered *I had felt something, lots of things actually,* when I had focused on his face.

My head throbbed. But the guy in my dream showed up for real in the stack of photos. I hadn't imagined him.

So, who was *he*?

I crumpled the corner of my napkin in between my fingers. What about the hammer? *The music guy had used his bare hands?* My body sunk into the seat. What kind of group home for mentally ill residents would have hammers? Wouldn't a hammer be considered a weapon? How could I have been so stupid and not thought of the logic in that?

Oh my God. What if the cops had believed me and arrested the wrong person? Why was I so sure I was right?

"You okay?" Dad asked, before he dipped a French fry into a mound of ketchup.

My heart raced. "So, it wasn't who I said?" I asked, as if I needed further confirmation of my inaccuracy. Blood rushed to my cheeks.

"No, of course not," Dad said. He looked away for a moment, like he was processing something before he took another swig of soda. Then, he set the drink down on the table, swirling the glass in his hands.

I stared at the small grooves in the booth behind my father's head.

How could I have been so wrong?

"What?" Dad asked, taking another bite of food. "Why are you upset? I thought you'd be pumped. Denise is gonna be fine."

I tightened my stomach. Why did the dream show me that man? Was that even possible, to mix up someone for somebody else? What was the point of my seeing a person who didn't commit the crime?

"Why are you taking this so personally?" Dad asked, his eyes small, back to the way they looked when he was in control.

"I just, I-I can't believe the dream was wrong—that I was wrong," I said, staring straight ahead into the back of the booth, the pattern becoming a blur. Applause broke out after a group of waitresses sang Happy Birthday to someone's relative, the sound as if it were happening in some faraway place.

"Did you honestly think your dream would solve Denise's case?" Dad asked. His shoulder twitched. "C'mon. Len looked blown away when you described the friggin' kitchen in the resident home. I think you'd just feel good about that. What else did you want out of it?"

Heat spread through my body like wildfire. "But what good did it do?"

Dad held his burger in mid-air. "What do you mean?"

"I mean, what good did it do?" I asked. A lump formed in my throat. "I saw Denise get hurt, badly hurt, and I saw the guy, except it wasn't the guy? What solid information is that?"

I stared down my plate of uneaten food.

"What were you hoping for?" Dad asked. He deliberately lowered his head as if to study me. "What'd you think you could save her or something?"

I continued to stare at the stack of French fries on my plate, slowly becoming cold. "I just wanted something good to come out of it. That's all."

I wanted it to mean something. Maybe a skill I could use for my future.

250

Dad swiped the side of his mouth with his napkin. "Let's focus on the fact that the cops got the guy, and now Denise's family can move forward with pressing charges or whatever. Tina said it'd make the six o'clock news. We can watch while you finally eat your food."

Ten minutes later, the flat screen TV above the bar flashed to the local news. Dad continued to eat his mushroom and cheddar burger while a spokesperson for the Hanley Police informed the public that Lars Thompson, who resided at the Hanley group home and had been off his medication, had been apprehended for the brutal beating of Denise Franklin.

No comment was given by Denise's family. Only a statement read by the officer that Denise, though still in the hospital, would make a full recovery and that her family was grateful to the Hanley police for the assailant's capture.

I slowly chewed bites of my cheeseburger as the screen switched to a slew of Hanley officers, standing off to the side of the platform where the spokesperson addressed the media. Bobby Dempsey flanked Len Dyer, on the far end of the television screen.

Dad pushed back his plate and asked, "Feel any better?"

My eyes still on the television screen, I sipped my ginger ale through the clear plastic straw. I noticed Bobby squinting at the end of the row, in the light of the setting sun that hit the front of the police station. "Sure," I muttered, not wanting to share that I found it hard to believe that that was it. Nothing was really solved in my mind, if I was being honest. Things still didn't make sense as to why this whole thing happened in the first place.

The news switched to a reporter at Fenway Park, covering David Ortiz's last season with the Red Sox.

"BTW, he's too old for you," Dad stated, before taking another swig of his soda. He gestured for the waitress with his finger along with a wink to bring the check.

I looked directly at my father and asked, "Who?" Then added with a smirk, "Len?"

Dad chuckled and moved his plate to the end of the table, clearly enjoying the banter of an entirely different subject. "You know who I mean," Dad said. He yanked two twenties from his brown leather wallet. "That younger cop at the station, but not young enough to go out with my high school daughter."

I raised my eyebrow. "And who indicated that was even a possibility?"

"Your old man is smart that way," Dad said. "C'mon, let's go home and put this whole thing behind us now that we know Denise is gonna be okay. You're a good kid with some whacked-out dreams. Let's leave it at that."

I slid out of the booth and followed my father out of the pub, wondering if I had any other choice.

CHAPTER TWENTY-FOUR

The following morning at 8:30, after a restless night of sleep and no ability to recall several fragmented dreams, I realized I had slept through calculus and second-period study, both of which didn't matter anyway. After a few moments, I sat up on the edge of my bed and flipped to the back page of the Intuitive Development packet that Randi had distributed during the workshop. I grabbed my cellphone and dialed Randi's number.

"Randi Miller," the curt, business-like voice answered on the second ring. Birds chirped in the background.

I paused first, my breath catching in my throat. "Hi, Randi, this is Devon Alante. I was in your workshop at the psychic fair. I don't know if you remember me, I was the only kid in the class. Well, teenager."

I heard the sound of a chair being dragged against a wooden floor. "Yes, Devon, I remember you. I thought you were a client calling me before our scheduled time. What can I do for you this early in the morning?"

I sat with one leg under me, digging my heel into the back of my thigh, while I sat on my bed. "I, I want to know why I would dream about something and feel like I was right, like one hundred percent right, and then, well, aspects of the situation happened, but it wasn't the person I saw. I mean, one of the people involved was right, the one it happened to, but not the person on the other end of things. It's, it's kind of difficult to explain. I'm just curious as to why I would see something so clearly and then find out that the information was wrong. That the person involved wasn't the person. Does that make sense? I mean, there were some things I got kind of right, it's just that those things didn't really count, or matter much." I exhaled, the muscles in my chest tight. I must have sounded like a chaotic mess. I couldn't even understand what *I* was saying.

"Ok, hold on. You said there were parts of your dream that ended up happening, yes?" Randi asked. I pictured her blinking on the other end of the phone.

"Yes," I answered. "But not the main piece, the person responsible. Why would I see someone who didn't even do what I saw them do in my dream? What does that mean?"

Randi covered the receiver, speaking to someone who sounded like it might be her husband and then said to me, "Do you remember when I said I had a dream about my brother's girlfriend being in the car?"

"Yeah," I replied.

"Okay, well, in the dream—and I didn't get into this during class because that would have taken longer—the girl I saw in the passenger side wasn't actually my brother's girlfriend. She was some girl I had never seen before and maybe never will. In fact, if I recall correctly, the girl in the dream wasn't even in his age range. But what matters, is that in the dream I sensed that she *represented* his girlfriend. How the details present themselves at times is not up to us to decipher and analyze. Look, for every number that shows up in my dreams, it's not like I'm going to go out and play the lottery. Though I think my husband is still waiting for it to work that way."

I twitched my toes, my forehead tight, trying to make sense of Randi's explanation in my mind.

"My point, Devon, without asking you to give me all the details of your dream because I have to go in a moment, is that sometimes things act as a metaphor in our dreams, versus a literal explanation. And that's often the hardest part. That can often become clearer—though not always—over time. What's important as a budding intuitive is that you had some parts to your dream that were validated. Right?"

I bit my lip. "Just the place where it all went down."

"Ok, well, that alone is thrilling. Hold onto that. We intuitives require validation. It helps us to keep doing what we're doing. Heck, as human beings we require validation. Validation is everything, besides safety."

I rolled my bottom lip, staring at the bunched-up covers on my bed.

"Before I hang up, did this help?" Randi asked.

"I think so," I said, trying to be satisfied about the fact that I did get the part about the kitchen right, and the attack. Even though I still had mixed feelings about not saying something.

"Good. Remember, literal versus metaphorical interpretation. That's the hardest part. Okay?"

I nodded and said, "Okay." I knew Randi had to go and I didn't want to overstep my boundaries.

"Just keep practicing the techniques. If you really want to do this, you've got to trust the information, even if it doesn't make sense to you. Often, my dear, it makes perfect sense to someone else."

I thanked Randi and hung up, gathering more information in my mind. I pulled at a thread in my bedding for a few minutes, listening to the elementary school busses drive past, before deciding to stay home for the rest of the school day.

CHAPTER TWENTY-FIVE

Later that night, as Dad stuffed take-out containers in the trash after supper and I sat at the kitchen table attempting to catch up on biology homework I had missed as a result of staying home, there was a crisp knock at the door.

"Hey, Len," I heard Dad say in a surprised tone after he opened the door. Then I heard Dad tell the detective that of course he could come in, that he was welcome anytime.

I glanced up, holding my pencil a few inches off the table. Dry leaves scattered across the back deck in the dark.

Dressed in his navy-blue windbreaker and dark blue pants, his round belly protruding out like a snowman's, Detective Dyer entered the kitchen. "Hi, Devon," Len said, raising his palm mid-air. "Might I speak with you for a few minutes? I won't take too much time away from your studies."

Please do, I thought, setting my pencil atop the over-erased blue-lined page in my notebook. My heart pitter-pattered inside me like a butterfly flapping its wings. Was Len here to make it a point that I got the wrong guy or something? I didn't feel like being embarrassed, especially in front of my father.

"Have a seat, Len," Dad said, gesturing toward the table. Dad stood beside the island, the lines around his eyes crinkled, appearing as confused as I was as to why Detective Dyer stopped by the house.

Len pulled out the chair at the head of the table, beside mine, and sat his hadn't-worked-out-since-before-he-took-this-job frame down in the frayed, straw-cushioned chair. "It's been quite busy, as I'm sure you can imagine, but I wanted to stop by briefly to talk to you and your father."

I pulled down the hem of my moss-green long sleeve and gripped the sheer fabric between my left thumb and first finger.

"I mentioned to you before," Len said, clasping his hands atop the table, his intense Irish blue eyes penetrating my own, "I've come to believe in these things, what you saw in your dream. Now, I have to be careful, young lady, and I can't give you credit, but I can confirm a few things on Denise's case that I felt you should know. That you deserve to know, and that, quite honestly, caught our department's attention."

Dad put back the liter of soda that had been on the island counter and then leaned against the closed refrigerator, gnawing on his lip as if he had an itch.

My heart soared around my chest, the way a point of light does when you swirl a flashlight against the wall.

Len sat back in the chair and tilted his head, making me feel as if this was an interrogation. "Although you didn't identify the person who attacked Denise in the queue of photos, what you described had enough accuracies to be what we call a hit."

I felt a lump form in my throat. "I don't understand."

Dad stepped over to the table, stood slightly beside my chair.

"Denise had a recent break-up with the man you identified," Len leaned his short forearms on the table. "That man you saw was her boyfriend—and although it didn't occur exactly the way you saw in your dream, Denise had threatened suicide after he broke it off. She wrote something in her journal that her mother found. I wrote it down so I could read it to you." Len took a ratty piece of paper out of the pocket of his shirt and unfolded its creases. Then he read from the torn page. "He might as well have taken a hammer to my heart, crushing it down until it flattened, like a pancake, barely able to continue beating." Len refolded the paper, holding it in his hand. "The hammer part you got wasn't so far off, in terms of her feelings."

I stared at the reddened knuckles on Len's hand, the gold wedding band on his finger shining in the light above the kitchen table. A lightness occurred in my chest. The hammer, *a metaphor.* Along with the fact that Denise liked to journal, like I did.

"But she got beaten up by the other guy," Dad interjected. He gripped the spindles on the back of the chair beside me.

"She did, yes," Len said, holding up his hand, "which I also want to talk to you both about."

I looked at Len, my eyebrows squished together.

259

"You mentioned a ring," Len's eyes narrowed as they pierced mine. "I had my guys specifically look for that piece of potential evidence in their search. That was a pretty specific detail, a silver skull ring. Well, we found it, young lady, in the trash. Denise's blood smeared on it, after we contacted Chase's trash pick-up service."

My lips parted. I curled my toes into the floor to feel something secure.

"When we asked the staff members who it belonged to," Len continued, "they identified Lars Thompson."

A dizzying feeling encompassed my head, like a swarm of bees surrounding me. I thought for a moment that I might pass out, yet the feeling was different than my regular dizzying feel of panic. I stared at the vertical ridges on the side of the salt and pepper shakers, hoping Dad might say something, but he remained silent.

"Devon?" Len asked, leaning in. "You good?"

I turned to Len, unable to speak.

"You identified a key piece of evidence, which helped lead us to Denise's attacker. Your dream contributed to collecting the puzzle pieces of a profile, necessary in an investigation. Now, I'm not saying we wouldn't have found the ring, because searching the trash is part of protocol. But when you gave those details, my ears perked up. That was a specific thing we could look for, to aid our search."

I felt the intense energy around my head redistribute downward, toward my toes. It felt like a pressure dam releasing inside me, perhaps for the first time. I wanted to sit in the feeling alone for a few more minutes.

"Her information helped your guys figure out the case?" Dad asked. His voice cracked as if he was speaking to a ghost sitting in Len's seat instead of a guy he had known for years.

"Sure did," Len said. "Though you can't quote me. Like I said, I can't give you credit, cause things don't work that way. What I can give you, though, is information. There's something called remote viewing, a subject we're learning more about at the department and potentially bringing in to our work. It's an area of investigative analysis I'm just learning about now at the ripe old age of fifty-four. Remote viewing considers the kind of data you provided as important. After speaking with you, I saw the process unfold real-time. I have to say, it made me more of a believer. To be perfectly candid, I shared this whole thing with my wife, who also happens to be into angel card readings and all that jazz. Liz is the one who encouraged me to come speak with you."

Dad twitched his shoulder, cracked his neck.

"There's something else though, too," Len said. He tapped the table with his pointy finger.

I felt my pulse rise.

"You mentioned the number twelve, something about the number twelve, do you remember that?"

I nodded, my face flushed.

"Lars Thompson, we found out, was given the nickname Twelve by the other residents. Twelve being the number of medications he took on a daily basis. The staff had even taken to calling him by that name. When we found the ring and asked who it belonged to, the nurse practitioner said, 'That's Twelve's.'"

Twelve. The number that wouldn't leave me alone. The number I thought that pertained to the stairs.

My father exhaled through his nose.

"I apologize I didn't let you or your dad know sooner. My plate's been a little full," Len said with a chuckle, "but I wanted to confirm your hunches, and let you know about the subject of remote viewing."

Dad cleared his throat, rubbed at his chin. "You really think there's something to this, Len?"

Len rapped his knuckles on the table. "Too close for comfort, in my opinion. I'll tell you a story. This elderly lady, Nadine was her name, she used to call the station from time to time, asking to be used as a resource on cold cases. I didn't think anything of it. Blew it off as nonsense. But one time, she emailed me with some information she said she got psychically after reading about a robbery in town in one of the local papers. She gave the guy's name, the town she felt he was from, the kind of car he drove, and a few other details—none of which panned out, as I had expected. Except for this one little detail, that ended up staying in my mind once we solved the case a month later. Nadine, who had since passed away, said she saw a royal blue and white printed bandana in the woods. Well, sure enough, we found that same bandana in the woods behind the guy's apartment complex. Now, it didn't solve the case, but when you're searching for leads, anything that helps point you in the direction, well, that's something to be considered. That's how I've come to look at it, anyway. After that, I kept Nadine's information on file. I actually called her a couple of times when we were stuck and I felt we could use a fresh perspective. She helped me on one other case after that—

locating a kid after he skipped probation. She told me to look at a burger restaurant in the plaza on Commercial Street. The kid didn't work there, but he ended up working two doors down at the hardware store. See, she pointed us in the right direction. I've started to realize that might be how this stuff works. You right-brain types showing us left-brain types a different way to look at things. Anyway, that's my take on it."

Dad rubbed at his forehead, his left hand still gripping one of the spindles on the chair.

"I hope that answers your question, PJ. In my humble opinion, I think you have something here, young lady. If I may be so bold, I also think you need to develop it, which leads me to the other reason I'm here and why I told you about the whole remote viewing thing." Len leaned forward in his chair while I bit the side of my thumb. "A woman is coming to teach remote viewing to a group of detectives and police officers at the department next spring. It's a workshop designed to access the non-local part of your brain, is what the pamphlet said, the place where dreams and intuition comes from, I guess. Accessing and understanding the subconscious, Carl Jung jargon. Which I remember a little bit from college, but not much, since I spent most of my time in the bars. Anyway, we thought you might get something out of it, learn a few things and potentially develop this skill further—if you're interested, and if your dad says it's okay. It'd be two nights a week, in the evenings, but I'll let you know the details as it gets closer."

I could barely stay seated. "This is perfect. I'd love to do that." Then, turning to my father, I asked, "You're okay with it, right?"

Dad scratched at the back of his hair. "I-I don't know. I gotta think about that, you're in school, and you work and—"

My eyes widened. "I hate serving ice cream. I want to learn more about this. What's the problem? Besides, I could still work at Holly's the other nights, if it's about the money." Suddenly, dealing with customers and having to endure small talk seemed a lot easier if I knew I was doing something more meaningful.

Dad dragged his hand over his face. "I told you I gotta think about this. I'm kinda getting sideswiped here."

Len slid back his chair. "Take all the time you need. We're talking months from now. I just have to make sure the funds are there for the participants. I'd need a little time to make a case for Devon to get on the class roster. You two talk it out and let me know. Well, I don't want to keep you from your studies. I'll let you get back to what you were doing, young lady. Liz has a nice roast waiting for me since I'm finally getting home at a normal hour this week." Len pressed his hands on his thighs before he stood. "Any questions before I head out?"

I looked up at Len. "So, I'm not one of those cat weirdos?"

Len feigned looking around. "You don't have a cat, do you?"

I smiled through pursed lips as Len pulled up the waist of his pants. "Now I know I don't have to worry about you posting this conversation on Facebook or other social media."

I shook my head. "I don't do Facebook."

"Good for you," Len nodded, patting the side of my right shoulder before he shook my father's hand to leave. "I knew I liked you, Devon, and not just because you're an Alante."

CHAPTER TWENTY-SIX

Two months later, on December 20, my birthday arrived under quiet, snowy-white conditions. Similar, I heard, to the day I was born. After having dinner with my family and friends at a local restaurant, we headed back to Avo's for dessert. Seated at the head of the mahogany dining room table, I watched as the wax dripped down from the seventeen glowing candles atop the vanilla cake with chocolate frosting my grandmother had made special for the occasion.

Avo rotated the string of pearls around her neck at the opposite side of the table, laughing along with my father—who sat to my right with his arms crossed over his dark-blue, long-sleeve shirt—and Uncle Rob, who sat on the other side of Dad, telling some funny story that happened to him and my father back in high school. Across the table, Frankie and Gwen listened to the stories, grinning as they likely compared my family's high school happenings to their own.

I considered what to wish for before I blew out the burning candles. I reflected on the day, how Dad had yelled up to Old Man Coleman watching us from his upstairs window that it was his "kid's seventeenth birthday!" before we got in the truck and headed to dinner. As wax melted into the dark frosting, I thought about how Mr. Coleman, and his house, still gave me the creeps for whatever reason. I didn't share that with my dad, though, on the way to dinner. My father had finally agreed to let me take the remote viewing class, as long as I kept the subject of my dreams, and "everything that went along with it," to myself.

I tucked my legs under my chair, fighting the urge to swing them back and forth in front of me the way I did when I was little. I thought about Denise who, after making a full recovery, had started back at the Natural Grocer at the beginning of December. The bruises on Denise's face had faded over the past two months. I noticed the traces of blue and greenish-yellow diminish every time I stopped in at the store, blaming my more frequent visits on the new dark chocolate and almond protein bars Tina kept in stock. I never confessed to the real reason I was there.

The television in Avo's living room, always on the cooking stations, murmured in the background. Denise received justice, and I felt grateful for that. Lars Thompson received a two-year jail term, a reduced sentence in exchange for being compliant with his medication—a condition Denise's family requested, because they were those kind of people.

Things turned out okay for me, too. Being offered the chance to study something I was interested in, and that a real detective thought I had a skill worth developing—something my teachers would never have figured out at school—made me realize that the definition of success was different for everyone.

I smiled to myself, imagining telling my classmates someday that I helped people by using my intuition—my clairvoyance, my clairaudience, my clairsentience abilities. I didn't care if someone judged me as being different or weird because I'm not like other kids in my class. I'm not.

I'm me.

And I am different, just like my classmates are different from me, with their likes and dislikes, talents and skills, and passions all their own. And now that I found *my* skills and *my* talents, that fact alone made me feel like I already achieved something in its own right. With all due respect to the five gifts waiting to be opened on Avo's freshly polished table, that really was the best seventeenth birthday gift I could receive.

Even though the dreams still scared me, and I didn't know where they came from or who wanted me to see them, I felt like I had at least figured out that the nightmares happened for a reason, and that they might be someone else's blessing.

After my dad told me to blow out my candles already, I brushed a strand of hair that had fallen into my face from behind my shoulder. My heart fluttered at the idea of being on Christmas break, of being halfway done junior year, of being excited about taking the class at the police station in the spring.

I closed my eyes and thought about Gram, and my mother, and how I still didn't know as much as I wanted to. Why she got to a point in her life that it ended the way it did. Why my father continued to keep things from me, that at my age I felt I should know. In my mind's eye, I imagined what my mother might look like at the table right now—and if it would be totally different from her young, long-haired, smiling self like in the picture Avo kept on the living room bookcase of my dad, mom and me at the restaurant after my baptism. If she was still here, I wondered how she would dress, how she might have sat beside my father if they stayed together. What she might have said to me on my seventeen birthday, how things had turned out for me.

I inhaled, deciding that if the point of the anxiety I had this past year, and during my whole life really, is that I'm supposed to learn from it and help people by using my intuition—however it shows up, and wherever it comes from—I could do that. Especially if, as a result, I'd be able to see Bobby Dempsey on a more frequent basis. Yeah, I could do that.

Suddenly, an image appeared in my mind. The little girl, in the room alone, making her appearance, in a flash, the way a light can go on and off in the matter of an instant. Did that mean I had made peace with the little girl, with the part of me that felt scared and alone? Or was there more about her that I needed to know?

Frankie drummed the table with his hands, in anticipation.

I made my wish and blew out my candles.

ACKNOWLEDGMENTS

Rebecca McCarthy, my editor, who cares about my characters, and the intention of my work, almost as much as I do. Working with you continues to motivate and inspire me.

Jody Amato for copy editing and positive encouragement, Janica Smith for publishing assistance, Clarissa Marcee for proofreading, and Yvonne Parks, who once again created a powerful cover.

Michael Bailey and Kate Jackson, fellow writers, friends and first readers for your valued feedback and contributions to Devon.

Laurie, my confidant, for your unwavering support of my work and just being you.

To the young clients I see who have incredibly powerful dreams and visions—stay the course, your strengths and insight as a result of this connection to something greater, will help make this world a better, more unified place.

Carl, for your read of my first draft early morning on a Cape Cod beach, the way you spoke of my characters, and the story itself, made me smile in my heart.

Carl, Kyle and Michelle, your support of my writing time is my special treasure. You are the foundation of my world.

Finally, for the dream experiences I've had from that other place since I was a young girl, and for feeling like things are coming full circle, I am grateful.

ABOUT THE AUTHOR

Photography by Maura Longueil

Jill Sylvester is an author and therapist in private practice. She lives outside Boston, Massachusetts with her family and their mischievous, yet adorable (third) bulldog. *Awakening* is her third book and first fictional series.

To contact Jill, visit her website at jillsylvester.com.

f fb.com/jill.sylvester.771

@jill_sylvester

@jillsylvester1

The Land of Blue

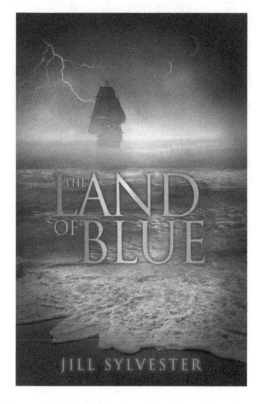

A young adult novel (for both kids and adults!) that takes readers on a fantastical voyage filled with hidden meaning, metaphors and messages, arriving at the destination of greater social and emotional well-being.

A wonderful tool for parents to read alongside their younger children.

The Land of Blue makes for powerful, thought-provoking discussion for middle and high-schoolers in both English and Wellness classrooms.